Stitched Up

Other books by Joanne O'Connell

Beauty and the Bin

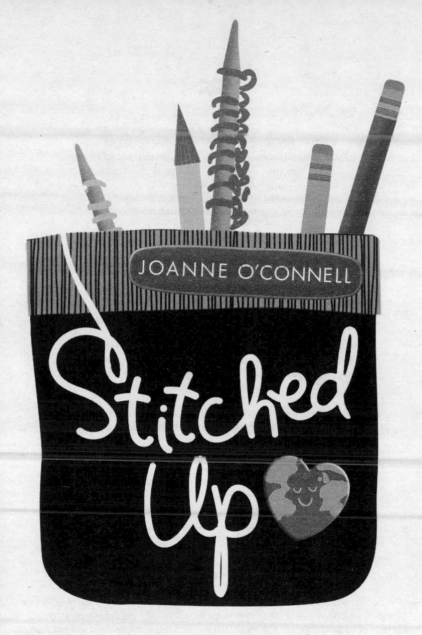

JOANNE O'CONNELL

Stitched Up

MACMILLAN CHILDREN'S BOOKS

Published 2024 by Macmillan Children's Books
an imprint of Pan Macmillan
The Smithson, 6 Briset Street, London EC1M 5NR
EU representative: Macmillan Publishers Ireland Ltd, 1st Floor,
The Liffey Trust Centre, 117–126 Sheriff Street Upper
Dublin 1, D01 YC43
Associated companies throughout the world
www.panmacmillan.com

ISBN 978-1-5290-3259-8

1 3 5 7 9 8 6 4 2

A CIP catalogue record for this book is available from the British Library.

Printed and bound by CPI Group (UK) Ltd, Croydon CR0 4YY

For Mum and Dad, with love x

'No one is without difficulties, whether in high or low life, and every person knows best where their own shoe pinches.'

— *Abigail Adams*

Chapter 1

Cassie smacked the palm of her hand against her forehead. 'If there was one day I should have got things right, it was today. I can't believe this is happening to me!'

'Like you couldn't believe you forgot your PE kit last week or that you hadn't done your Maths homework?' said her sister Emily, who was two years older than Cassie. 'Or that you'd left your coat tied around a tree trunk on the playing field—'

'This is completely different. It really matters!' said Cassie, breathlessly. She jumped up from her bus seat.

Emily pulled her back. 'Stop acting like it's an emergency! It's not the end of the world to wear your school uniform on wear-your-own-clothes day.'

'But it is! A fashion emergency is literally *the worst*!'

Cassie wailed. 'Azra says that the first non-uniform day of our high school career is the biggest of our lives. That it's basically our *fashion debut*.'

Emily rolled her eyes. 'Azra says a lot of things . . .'

Cassie looked out of the bus window. It was quarter-past-eight in the morning and already the bus had reached the pizza place on the outskirts of the village. That meant they had ten minutes, tops, before they pulled up outside Pipson High School.

'But there's nothing you can do now so just try and—'

'Focus,' said Cassie, loudly. She tried to ignore how fast her heart was beating. 'I've got to focus and think of something fast.'

'I don't really see what—'

'Because there is NO WAY that I am going into school dressed like this.'

Cassie pulled at her school skirt. *It's called non-uniform day for a reason*, she told herself, furiously. *NON-uniform!* Her mind raced. She thought about her favourite fashion-history creators. The ones who posted

2

hacks to put a spin on what they were wearing. Old shirts were repurposed into sixties' mini dresses; pairs of tights upcycled into 1930s' style headbands. There had to be a way to elevate her outfit. There *had* to be.

Her brain threw up an image of the first ever school uniform from back in the 1550s. If she put her coat on and wrapped her tie around her waist like a sash, she'd look like a Tudor schoolgirl. Yes, technically she'd still be in uniform. But it was a serious style twist . . .

Emily looked worried. 'You need to do that breathing-through-your-nose-and-out-through-your-mouth thing.'

Cassie covered her face with her hands. 'Today's going to be as bad as ' Cassie felt a surge of humiliation as she remembered that last week she'd misread her timetable and gone to a swimming lesson when she should have been in Spanish. She'd done half a length of the pool before a girl in another form pointed out that she was in the wrong place. Cassie had jumped out, panic-dressed, and raced, dripping wet, to the classroom. The whole class had exploded with laughter.

Emily gave Cassie a friendly shove. 'Wet Spanish? Or remember when you wore those flowery knickers as a hat to my birthday party?'

'I was three, Emily!'

Emily delved into her bag for her breakfast. 'You have to calm down. Remember what we said about trying to relax on the bus?' She tore a cinnamon bun in two and gave Cassie half.

'And now all that money I spent on that sweatshirt dress is wasted.' Cassie's shoulders did an involuntary shiver.

'You should have worn your 1920s' flapper dress.' Emily bit into the bun.

Cassie felt a sharp jab of pain, like she'd pricked her finger with a needle. She didn't want to think about how much she wished she was wearing that dress.

Cassie loved fashion history. Whenever she couldn't sleep at night, she recited the timeline of frocks, from funky beadnet dresses (high fashion for the Egyptians), to eighteenth-century elaborate hoop skirts, to the Y2K dresses-over-jeans trend (what was everyone thinking?!).

She loved wearing clothes from different eras, and pulling everything together with jeans, bracelets and hair scarves. She had a genuine sixties' mini skirt that used to be her gran's; an eye-catching vintage brooch, and a top with puff sleeves (from a second-hand clothes app, but it looked oh-so Georgian).

And her *pièce de résistance* was a shimmering gold 1920s'-style cocktail dress, which her parents had given her for her twelfth birthday. It had an iconic drop waist, crystal droplets around the neckline, and sparkly fringes in a zig-zag pattern, which gave it an irresistible swish as she moved.

At home, Cassie liked to go 'Full Flapper' and dance around the flat in the dress with her mum's scarf tied into her bobbed hair, and a string of classic pearls. For non-uniform day, though, she'd planned to wear the twenties' dress like a pinafore, with a tee underneath, and her chunky trainers. Timeless with a twist: the perfect example of Cassie's fashion-history aesthetic.

But Azra had said NO WAY. According to Azra, letting people know you were a hundred years behind the fashion curve was one of the biggest mistakes you could make at high school.

Cassie's best friend Azra was warm, friendly and excitable. She had a thick fringe she could flip up and down like a stage curtain, and although they'd only met at the start of term three weeks ago, she and Cassie were already super-close. They ate their lunch together, messaged each other constantly, and whenever the teacher asked them to work in twos, she and Azra would immediately pair off.

But Azra was also impressively blunt.

In the canteen the other day, Cassie had excitedly announced that she was going to wear her twenties' dress for non-uniform day, and Azra had screamed. '*Anything* but that!'

And when Cassie came up with other ideas (like

her sixties' skirt from her gran) Azra said she was waaaaaaay off track. She told Cassie that *she* would find her something to wear. It was crucial to get it right, according to Azra, because today wasn't only a non-uniform day; it was the launch of a new project for year sevens.

No one knew the details (there was going to be a big announcement in Assembly later) but the rumour was it was something to do with fashion. And if that was true, then it was more important than ever to get their non-uniform day looks exactly right.

'Azra said if we both wore sweatshirt dresses for non-uniform day, it would not only show the power of our friendship, it would create a "fashion moment".'

'You've only *known* each other a moment!' Emily brushed some crumbs off her skirt.

Cassie flinched. Who cared how long it had been? When you knew, you knew. And from the first moment Cassie had walked into 7B's form room and Azra had leapt up yelling 'Hair Twins!' – she and Cassie both had plaits to the side of their heads – she knew they would be friends for ever.

But now Cassie cringed thinking about how excited Azra had been about the sweatshirt dresses, snapping up the lavender 'fit as soon as it went on sale and instructing Cassie to get it in grey.

It had only just been Cassie's birthday, so there was no way she could ask Mum and Dad to buy her the dress, but when Cassie's mum heard about the 50%-off sale she offered Cassie an advance on next month's allowance. Seconds later, Cassie had screen-grabbed the words: *your order is complete!* and sent them to Azra, who responded with new links, this time to pineapple pendants and cherry earrings and the words: 'time to accessorize!!!!!'.

Now though, Cassie's hand flew to her neck. 'What's Azra going to say when she sees I'm not even wearing any fruit jewellery?'

'Message her,' Emily said, firmly. 'It'll give her time to process the shock, which means we won't have to see her self-implode at the gates.'

Suddenly the bus jolted forward. Cassie's head jerked up to the window. They'd reached the crossroads, opposite the pub, which meant they were a minute away from the shiny copper-and-glass buildings of Pipson High School for Girls swinging into sight.

Cassie's brain snapped into focus.

She yanked her PE kit onto her lap and pulled out her trainers. She shoved them on. There had to be something else she could wear, there just *had* to be. She tipped her satchel upside down. Was there any chance she had a spare tee-shirt? Pencils, sandwiches, fruit, biscuits and books fell all over the bus seat.

'What are you doing?' Emily scrambled around, picking things up.

'Looking for a paper bag to put over my face. I need something to cover me up so that no one—'

As the bus lurched around the corner, Cassie nearly lost her balance. She grabbed her sister's arm to steady herself. Emily was wearing a shirt so thick it was nearly a jacket and it was so baggy that Emily hardly noticed when Cassie yanked it.

Wait!

Cassie stared at her fistful of fabric. Emily's shirt-come-jacket was so oversized it was basically a tent. Cassie's heart pounded. *I could wear pyjamas, or a bikini, or even nothing at all under that*, she thought, *and no one would be able to tell*. She'd literally be hidden in plain sight.

This was PERFECT.

She moved faster than she ever had in her entire life. Within seconds, she'd tucked the collar of her shirt down and tied the laces of her trainers. She whipped off her tie.

Emily did a double take. 'What's going on?'

'I need to borrow your shacket!'

Emily threw it over.

'Thank you!' Cassie's fingers desperately ran up and down its sides, trying to find the zips, buttons or press studs.

The bus was pulling up at the bottom of the school driveway. Emily was sweeping up the rest of Cassie's books and snacks.

Emily grabbed Cassie's arm and hauled her down the steps, just in time.

As they ran towards the gates, Cassie felt a burst of confidence. No wonder people said shackets were an essential hero piece! *You could dance in a storm wearing this*, she thought. *You could battle a blizzard.*

It was swingy and joyful, and the colour! Golden yellow paired with a glossy block of red. Cassie hoped it made her warm chestnut hair and her hazel eyes shine. *And yes*, thought Cassie, *underneath I'm wearing school uniform. But no one will ever know.*

This is what you call being fashion fearless.

Emily opened the door of the student entrance.

'I want to give you a massive hug, Em, and say a proper thanks! But I can't let go of this until I find the fastenings—'

The door swung back and hit Cassie in the face. By

the time she'd rubbed her cheek and rearranged herself, so she had a free hand to push the door open again, Emily was halfway down the corridor.

'Wait! How do you do this thing up?'

'You can't!' shouted Emily, as she disappeared around the corner. 'It's a buttonless piece, remember? It's meant to hang loose!'

Cassie flattened her back against the wall of the corridor. Hang loose? What a TOTAL DISASTER! She caught sight of her reflection in the glass windows of the corridor. *OMG, I look like a walking beach towel.*

'Watch it!' said Holly and Bea as Cassie nearly smacked into them.

'Sorry,' said Cassie, automatically.

They eyed Cassie's shacket like a panther does its prey. Cassie pulled the sides more tightly together.

Holly and Bea were unnerving at the best of times. They called themselves The Populars and went around laughing at people and saying things like 'life's not perfect but your trainers should be'. *If we lived in Tudor times*, thought Cassie, *Holly and Bea would have loved public executions.*

Today, they were in sweatpants and statement pieces – they were into extreme high-low dressing. Bea had a necklace so sparkly it wouldn't look out of place in the crown jewels. Holly had an enormous fluffy jacket, which she trailed along the floor like it was a dog on a lead.

'It's not National Cosplay Day, by the way!' said Holly.

'Hahaha!' Bea sounded like fake audience laughter on TV. She smoothed her hands over her trademark slicked-back hair. 'Or is this your new aesthetic? I've heard *Cheese Core* is really in right now.'

Cassie's chest went tight with panic.

'You'd better Brie joking.' Holly's deep-set dark eyes were flashing. 'Tell me you are.' She put her hand on her hip. 'Holly needs to know.'

Cassie felt her cheeks burn.

'I was just on my way to . . .' Cassie nodded her head

in the direction of the loos. If she could just get there, she'd find a way to fasten her shacket. A kirby grip holding the top together might work. Sellotape down the middle? Worst-case scenario she could use her tie like a sash around her waist . . .

There was a moment of silence.

Bea tried to contain a laugh. 'To get some honey!'

'Honey?' Holly did a double take. Her long hair swished out so far that it nearly smacked Cassie's face. 'Tell me that you haven't dressed as Pooh Bear?'

'Of course I haven't dressed up as—'

Bea pointed at Cassie's top half. 'He wears that cropped red jacket and that shacket is yellow teddy fabric and it's so big that—' she broke off, as if she couldn't even finish the sentence, it was that funny.

Cassie tried to get past them. But she and Holly did that annoying thing where they both moved at the same time, and her way was blocked. 'Sorry,' she said, again.

Just as she thought they'd let her go, Holly scooped

her own coat up under her arm and made a show of opening the door. Cassie felt herself being shoved into the form room.

'People of 7B!' boomed Holly. 'Let's give a big welcome to a very special visitor from the Hundred Acre Wood . . .'

'Excuse me.' Before she could say anything else, an older girl pushed past them and went into the form room.

There was a sudden change in atmosphere.

The girl was Mira Lal.

Mira was in year eleven, with dramatic eyeliner, a Taylor Swift cardigan, and a super-cool reputation. She and her friend Bella (who had a guitar slung over her shoulder, and wore clogs that clattered on the school floors) were what Azra called corridor celebrities.

During lesson change, if Mira and Bella walked past, the year sevens spoke in awed tones: 'Did you see the paintings in Mira's Art folder?' Have you heard Bella play?' Even Holly and Bea instinctively held doors open for them, like they were teachers.

Bea did a little squeak and shot into her seat. Everyone else pretended not to stare. Holly hastily reapplied her lip gloss and went into hyper-enthusiasm mode. 'Can we help you with anything at all?'

'No thank you,' said Mira, sweeping past.

Cassie's heart skipped when she saw the beautifully knitted silver stars on Mira's cardigan sleeves.

'There it is!' Mira pulled a bright-yellow-and-red shacket off one of the painting easels near the window.

No one moved. Holly and Bea's mouths dropped open as they slowly looked from Cassie's shacket to the exact same one that Mira was now holding. Cassie held her breath.

'Left this in here yesterday,' Mira said. At the door, she flashed a smile to Cassie. 'Love your style, by the way!'

The second Mira was gone there was a loud scraping of chair legs on the floor. 'Let-me-see, let-me-see!' Azra was shrieking with excitement. She ran over to Cassie

and stroked her sleeve like it was a newborn puppy.
'You're so full of fashion surprises!'

Cassie flushed.

'You didn't tell me you were getting a jacket as well
as the sweatshirt dress!' Azra said, breathlessly. 'Wait,'
she rubbed her fingers on the fabric of Cassie's sleeve.
'Is it a jacket or is it a shirt?'

'I guess it's both!'

Azra looked really impressed. 'Wow, Cassie! I would
normally say that the colourways are way too much . . .'

– last week, when Cassie had worn a bright yellow
scrunchie, Azra had wailed 'GLARING!' and pretended
she needed sunglasses –

'. . . but if Mira Lal is wearing it—'

Cassie laughed. 'It's Emily's! It's her great taste, not
mine.'

'Well, it's both your great tastes,' said Holly, with
sudden friendliness. Bea nodded.

Cassie ignored them. She pulled her top around her
shoulders.

'Wait.' Azra's eyes suddenly narrowed. 'Why are you wearing it wrapped around you like that?'

Cassie did a little shiver. 'Just feeling cold.'

Azra's eyes flicked to the window. Warm September sunlight was pouring into the classroom.

Quick – change the subject! Cassie pointed to Azra's ears. 'Love your earrings! Cherries are so cool!'

Cassie swiped her phone. She'd researched cherry prints in retro fashion only the other day. She clicked on her images. Swingy skirts from the fifties; the famous cherry wiggle dress worn by a film star in the sixties; and a sensational frock from the end of the nineteenth century. Glossy cherries were beautifully embroidered onto realms of silk. She felt a rush of excitement. 'Look at this, Az! The pattern is just like your earrings. This dress was gifted by a princess to a museum in New York in the 1930s . . .'

'And these were gifted to me from my auntie only last week. She got them from Claire's.' Azra looked a bit put out. 'They're not hundreds of years old!'

'I wasn't saying—'

'They're brand new and on trend. Just like our sweatshirt dresses!'

Cassie shoved her phone back into her bag.

Azra suddenly jumped up. 'I've got an idea! Our dresses will create a real moment, we know that, but we can't waste this amazing shacket either.'

'It's OK. I'll keep it on.'

Azra shook her head. 'What I mean is, we need to *share* it, that way we both get the benefit. But we can still create a moment later on—'

'I can't just take it off . . .'

'Tell you what we can do.' Azra clapped her hands. 'We can have a Rota.'

'A Rota?'

'You can wear it for Maths, we've got that first lesson. I'll be in it for Drama. And break . . .'

'I think we should just stay as we are.'

'What's third lesson? French. OK, you could wear it then . . .'

'It's Emily's, though, I can't risk losing it.'

'We'll split lunch so we can both wear it when everyone's in the canteen. The place will be heaving. It's only fair if we both get to be seen in it . . .'

Cassie could feel the room beginning to spin. Emily had been right. She should have messaged Azra when they were on the bus. Telling her anything face to face was impossible. 'I think it's best if I keep the shacket on and—'

'Honestly, this is going to be so great.' Azra's green eyes were shining. 'I'm so excited that you've worn this! Just let me try it on before Mr Jackson gets here for registration.'

Cassie's stomach flipped. 'I'm cold right now and—'

Azra held her hand out. 'Quick!'

'Give her a break!' said a loud voice. 'How many times does she have to tell you she doesn't want to take it off?'

Cassie's head whipped around. Fern Larksie was sitting on a desk near the window. She was twisting paper clips into a hair slide to accessorize her outfit. She was wearing a handkerchief dress she'd made from scarves, and cowboy boots, which she'd rescued from landfill.

Fern had blazed into the form room on the first day of school, wearing a homemade uniform and delivering an impassioned speech about sweatshops, the planet-polluting fashion industry and how she wanted to kickstart a fashion revolution.

Azra rolled her eyes. 'Here we go . . .'

Fern put the slide in her hair. She looked up to see Cassie looking at her. She grinned. 'I saw the price of some slides like this on Etsy the other day, and I thought, what the heck? That's basically wire and old ribbons! So, I thought I'd make one.' She did a funny walk, turning her head in a comic way so everyone could see the clip. 'From rubbish to runway . . .'

'It's rubbish alright,' murmured Azra, touching the side of her head. Azra had her trademark clips in every shade of purple.

'To other people, maybe!' Fern spun around. 'But to me, this trash is treasure.' She suddenly looked serious. 'But back to the fashion bullying—'

'It's a shacket,' said Azra.

Cassie's insides swirled. Bullying was maybe a bit strong.

'And it's not bullying. It's a private conversation,' said Azra. 'Between best friends.'

'But you're asking Cassie to publicly remove her shacket within the school setting,' said Fern. 'So, technically it's not private. And sorry, but you seemed a bit pushy, so I thought I'd step in and—'

'Interfere.' Azra sounded upset.

'I help out,' said Fern. She threw Cassie a supportive smile.

Azra turned to Cassie. 'All I've asked for is—'

Just then, the door swung open and their form teacher Mr Jackson strode in. 'Sit down! Thought I'd come in my casuals too,' he announced, as he plonked his bag on the desk. 'I might do it every Friday.'

Mr Jackson was wearing Dad jeans and a tee-shirt that read *'This is what a feminist looks like'* and trainers that looked like they'd time travelled from the early 2000s.

Holly's mouth dropped open. 'This is what a fashion crime looks like.'

There was a general murmur of agreement. Mr Jackson clapped his hands. 'You can thank me later for being the coolest form teacher ever,' he smiled, as he started the register.

An hour later, and Cassie had got through Maths (easy because Azra was in the set above her, so they weren't together) but the shacket now had a starring role in Drama.

They had been doing improvizations to a theme of Life on the Ocean Wave. Cassie was pretending to steer a boat over the sea in Scotland. She had one hand on the invisible wheel and another on the sides of the shacket, to keep it closed. She was pretending this was to keep out the driving rain. She'd been telling Fern how the shacket looked like the iconic yellow mac created by the Scots in the nineteenth century and Fern said to totally go for it.

Azra was a lighthouse on the rocks. She was frantically spinning around and around. Fern and a girl called Jules were pretending to be passengers riding the waves.

'It's beautiful out here,' said Jules, her hand on her eyebrows, scanning the imaginary water. 'I can see a whale!'

Cassie laughed. Jules was smiley, friendly and always in a good mood. Nothing got her down and when anyone else was down, she cheered them up with comedy videos of her cat.

'Take your mac off!' yelled Azra. 'Pretend it's flown off in the wind. Throw it on my head. The light will go out and you'll have to—'

'I can't take it off. I've got to steer this thing!' said Cassie, with feeling.

'Talk about immersive acting,' said Mrs Blych, the

Drama teacher. She grasped her hands to her chest. 'With that coat, I can really believe you're out there battling the waves...'

'This coat is EVERYTHING to me right now!' said Cassie, emotionally.

'How moving!' Mrs Blych got everyone to gather around. She explained that Cassie's coat showed how costumes can bring a performance to life. *It definitely brought Azra's facial expressions to life,* thought Cassie. *Her scowl could probably be seen from Scotland.*

The tension went up a notch at lunchtime. Carrying a bowl of pasta all the way from the canteen queue – through the shoving and noise – back to their seats beside the window was like doing an awkward dance. Cassie's arm was actually beginning to ache from the strain of holding her shacket together all day. She wished she'd bought a couple of milkshakes. At least she could have sucked them through a straw.

And outside, the September sunshine was filtering

down onto the field. As they walked around, everyone was taking off their top layers and enjoying the warmth. Cassie was hot and sweaty. She couldn't have felt more out of place if she was wearing a Christmas jumper on a boiling hot beach.

But she was doing a good job of pretending not to notice Azra's increasingly desperate attempts to share the shacket. Whenever it got super tricky, Cassie pretended to have a coughing fit, and had to turn around until the moment passed.

Now all she had to do was get through Assembly and she could go home.

'In a way, it's a good thing that you've kept the shacket on,' said Azra, as they walked to the hall.

They sat down. Cassie carefully wrapped the sides around her like a dressing gown.

'It means we can surprise everyone!'

'Surprise everyone?' Cassie's stomach flipped. The hall was filling up with over two hundred year sevens.

'When Ms Ginty announces the fashion project, you

can throw off the shacket and show you're wearing a sweater dress like me. The surprise is our fashion moment!' Azra paused, then forced a smile. 'And it'll be a surprise to me too because I've *still not seen you in it.'*

'Quiet, please!' said Mr Jackson.

Ms Ginty, the head of lower school, stepped onto the stage, giving off her usual sparkle and shine. Floaty ombre blouse, pastel-blue wide-leg trousers, glittery eye shadow, and a smile as radiant as a lead vocalist in a popular girl band, which once upon a time Ms Ginty had been.

Ms Ginty was a major part of Pipson High School's appeal. Along with everyone else, Cassie had seen the photos and videos of Ms Ginty (or *Ginty Fresh*, as she'd been known back then) as a pop star when she was young. And everyone knew about how the band had split; how Ms Ginty had reinvented herself as an owner of a chain of tea houses and later, after a well-publicized sale, she'd decided to switch track again and become a teacher.

One of the best things about Ms Ginty was that she was always upbeat. It was like there was a film crew following her around for a programme called *Is This Britain's Cheeriest Teacher?* But even by her high standards of cheeriness, Ms Ginty was fizzing with energy today.

'I'm excited – no, I'm electrified – to announce the new year-seven project, which – yes, the rumours are right! – is all about fashion.'

The tension was bristling off Azra. Her green eyes were flashing like traffic lights. 'Get ready,' she hissed to Cassie.

Ms Ginty flicked a switch. A slideshow of photos of girls wearing the Pipson High uniform came up on the big screen. 'Pleated skirts in the twenty-first century!' said Ms Ginty. 'Shirts and ties! Is this what we really want?'

An outbreak of excited murmuring went around the room.

Yes! Cassie screamed inwardly. *That is really what*

I want. The uniform was hands down one of the best things about starting year seven. Cassie loved everything about it from the pleated navy skirt to the silky striped tie. She hadn't been able to wait to get shot of her red primary school sweater and grey dress.

'I thought not! So, who wants to design a new uniform?'

Hands flew into the air. People were throwing out suggestions like a different-coloured top for each day of the week or workwear for English and Maths, boilersuits for Design Tech, costumes during History to match the era . . .

Azra was shifting about on her seat. 'This is supposed to be about *fashion*. No way am I wearing a medieval tunic!'

'How about maxi dresses?' shouted a girl called Mei, who was in another form. 'We could wear florals in summer!' She threw her arm out theatrically. 'And we could design a pattern with leaves and acorns for autumn . . .'

Azra nodded. 'That's more like it.' She turned to Cassie. 'When everyone sees our matching dresses, they'll see how on it we already are.'

'And a special party one for Christmas!' said Mei's friend Reeta.

Mei pointed her finger, approvingly. 'With sequins!'

'It's a no to the dresses,' Holly said equally loudly. She pulled at her joggers. 'Especially any with leaves on! Unless you want to be covered in squirrels on the field every lunchtime.'

Bea did her automatic laugh.

'But fluffy PJs or sweats?' said Holly. 'I'm here for that!'

Bea nodded. 'We need a low-key vibe for school on normal days.' She twirled her necklace in her fingers. 'Because there's nothing about this place that says party.'

After a minute or two, Ms Ginty did her trademark 'woo-hoo!' shout to get everyone's attention. 'Exciting, isn't it? Just think about the impact this could have.

According to all the research I've read, most of us only wear a small percentage of what's in our wardrobes. But that's not true of school uniform. You're in it five days a week! We need cosy, covetable clothes that are an everyday reminder of the stars that you are!'

'Get in!' Azra was ablaze. She turned to Cassie. 'Whoever designs the new uniform will be fashion famous! We've got to win this thing!'

Ms Ginty put her hand above her eyes as if she was scouting the crowd for interest. 'Anyone with an idea for a cool school aesthetic? Can anyone use a sewing machine? You can sketch out your design, but I reckon there'll be extra points if you make a prototype . . .'

Cassie wriggled around inside her shacket. Already her school clothes felt like a part of her. And she loved how it showed she belonged to Pipson, like all the girls across the ages who she'd seen in the school photos on the corridor outside the library.

She thought of the photo from the 1960s with girls wearing berets, the knitted tank tops that came in during the eighties, the oversized style of blazer in the early 2000s and the sweatshirts of the past few years. And through it all, the girls were united by the same basic uniform: navy blue pleated skirt, crisp white shirt, school crest on the blazer . . .

She imagined the next school photo on the wall of the corridor. Would everyone be in fluffy pyjamas?

She felt a rush of nerves. She knew a fashion design competition was exciting, but there was a big part of her that didn't want to change. *I'd go back to the berets and the blazers if I could . . .*

Ms Ginty explained how everyone had to get into pairs and work on a design. The school was looking for an affordable, inclusive, climate-friendly outfit that could take you from Maths to Music to Modern Languages.

They had three weeks. After that, there'd be a special Assembly to showcase the designs, and everyone would vote for their favourite.

'We'll need a couple of coordinators from year seven. Their job will be to encourage people to enter, and to make sure the designs are inclusive and affordable. But we can decide who can do that later . . .'

Bea and Holly's hands shot into the air.

Ms Ginty laughed. 'I think your hands were up before I finished that sentence!' She pointed at Holly and Bea. 'OK. You're our Fashion Coordinators! See me afterwards for the details.'

Cassie's heart dropped. There was no way anything would be left of the traditional uniform if *they* were involved. Holly would want everyone to wear coats the size of Old English sheepdogs. And as for *inclusive* and *climate-friendly*?

'Tell you what, I'm in a decision-making mood. So, let's decide on Team One! Our first Fashion Dream Team, if you like. I'm not saying that they're more likely to win – we want lots of you to enter – but we all know first impressions do count . . . So, anyone ready to team up?'

There was a loud cheer.

Azra whacked Cassie on the arm. 'Put your hand up!'

Cassie's heart was in her mouth. She was so close to the end of the day, there was NO WAY she could wreck things now.

She held her sleeve carefully and half-heartedly put her hand up, hoping it wouldn't be visible from the stage. For a second, Ms Ginty's eyes rested on her. Cassie pretended to have a coughing fit, so her hand came down. Ms Ginty's gaze moved on.

Phew. Cassie pulled her shacket around her so tightly it looked like she was hugging herself.

Suddenly, Fern was on her feet. 'I'll do it! I've already made my own uniform from fabric that would have gone to waste. I'm 100 per cent against fast fashion because In my opinion It wrecks people's lives as well as the climate.'

'And in my opinion, you need to sit down,' said Mr Jackson, tightly. He glared at Fern.

Fern pulled an apologetic face at him. 'Sorry, Mr Jackson, but the fashion revolution is calling! This project is bang on perfect for me because we need a new way of dressing ourselves while we're at school, and we need it now. We can use this redesign as a rallying cry for—'

'You'll be crying in a minute if you don't sit down. NOW!' Mr Jackson raised his voice.

Ms Ginty held her hand up. 'Thanks, Mr Jackson. Fern, you should listen to your form teacher . . .' There was a pause. Ms Ginty bounced up on her trainers for a moment. Finally, she said, 'But I can't think of anyone better to be in our very first team. So, Fern? It's a yes from me!'

Fern's face lit up with excitement as she made her way to the stage. Even when her homemade hair clip fell out as she went up the steps, she was still glowing as she stood next to Ms Ginty.

Azra was incandescent. 'This should be our moment! She's stolen our fashion surprise!'

'We have the first member of our Fashion Dream Team.' Ms Ginty looked at the sea of hands in the air. 'OK, Fern, you know your fellow year sevens better than me. Why don't you choose who you want to work with?'

Azra looked desperate. 'Remember, if she picks you, Cassie, you have to say no because we're already a pair.'

'She's not going to pick me!'

'Cassie Coltsfoot,' said Fern.

What?

Cassie's face went bright red. She felt everyone staring at her.

'Lovely! Up you come, please,' Ms Ginty gestured.

Cassie's heart was racing. There was a big lump at the back of her throat. She could feel the stress of the day about to explode inside her. This was too much, way too much.

Mr Jackson leant over towards them. 'Is there a problem?' he said, in a tone that made it clear there had better not be a problem.

Cassie swallowed. 'It's just that—'

'You can't do this without me. You can't just be on a team with Fern! What about me?'

'Come on now,' said Ms Ginty.

Cassie cleared her throat. 'I don't think I can—'

'—come alone!' said Azra, loudly. 'She can't work with you, Fern, because Cassie and I have already paired up!' She looked distraught. 'We're best friends and it's not fair if we are separated on a fashion project that's—'

'—that's meant to be fun, I agree! Maybe we shouldn't restrict everyone to pairs?' said Ms Ginty. She clapped her hands. 'Come on up, Cassie *and* Azra. Let's make this team a trio!'

Azra stood up so fast she nearly knocked her chair over. She grabbed Cassie's arm and yanked her towards the stage. It was all Cassie could do to keep one hand on the shacket and not trip up. The way Azra was dragging her along there was every chance she was about to fall flat on her face.

'Don't look so terrified!' said Ms Ginty. 'I love those bright colours. But if you're nervous, why don't you stand in the middle of your friends for the photo?'

'A photo?' said Cassie.

Take off the shacket,' Azra said, urgently.

Cassie's grip tightened. Ms Ginty was swiping the camera settings. Cassie's stomach did a nasty lurch. 'Az, I really—'

'Are you OK?' Fern looked worried. 'You look like you're going to be sick.'

'Now!' said Azra. 'This is our moment.'

'What I'm looking for is some real energy,' said Ms Ginty. 'Tell you what, can you hold hands and whip your arms up when I take the photo?'

Cassie felt every cell in her body slam into panic mode. 'I'm not sure I can—'

'One . . . two . . .'

'Three!'

As the camera flashed, Cassie's arms were whipped up high, like she was a puppet. Her shacket flew open. And captured on the big screen was the meme-able moment of Cassie in her school uniform, Azra's shocked face and the words: Meet the FASHION DREAM TEAM!

Chapter 2

The second Assembly was over, Cassie left the hall and ran home as fast as she could.

Cassie's phone was non-stop buzzing like it had been hacked by a spam account. She didn't want to see her messages. Not until she was home. She ran through the doorway of the flats and threw herself down onto the communal staircase.

There were eleven text messages, and a notification flashing about voice calls. She clicked that first. *You have two new messages.* The first one was from Emily, who had gone to after-school climbing club: 'Heard all about it. Five deep breaths! The emergency chocolate spread is in the cupboard where we keep the bin bags.' Cassie felt fresh panic. Her sister would only have told her about the chocolate spread if she considered this to be a MAJOR incident.

The next was from Fern: 'Wearing school uniform was an AMAZING statement! The most climate-cool thing to do is wear clothes you already have. And I don't know if this helps, but when I'm having a bad day I think about the polar bears on melting glaciers, and then I just get back out there.'

No, thought Cassie. *Sorry, Fern, but it 100% doesn't.* Now she was worrying about polar bears as well as how she'd shamed herself in front of the whole of year seven. In fact, what might have made her feel better was for Fern to not have got involved in the first place.

OK. Now for the texts. There was only one that wasn't from Azra.

Jules: **Smile. Don't worry!** ❤ ❤ ❤ **It's not as embarrassing as what my cat Bevan did on holiday!**

Jules sent a video

Cassie liked the video

Cassie: **Thank you!**

Cassie: **Even though what I've just done is nothing like as cute as Bev accidentally going down a water slide, I appreciate the thought!**

Azra: **I KNEW there was something weird about that shacket!!!!!!!!!**

Azra: **Knew it.**
But you need to EXPLAIN.
IDK what is going on?!!!!!!!

Azra sent a photo

> **Azra:** Have you SEEN the photo of us on stage? It's all over the 7B form chat.

> **Azra:** Did you not want the sweatshirt dress?

Then, when there was no reply, Azra seemed to get worried.

> **Azra:** Least tell me you're OK.

Oh no, thought Cassie. *I should have replied. This is what happens when you don't answer your phone.*

She quickly tapped out:

> **Cassie:** I'm OK.

But before she hit send, another one flew in.

Azra: Honestly great start to a fashion dream team or WHAT? It was meant to be our fashion debut not a fashion disaster.

Azra: Wait. Why was Fern sticking up for you this morning? Don't you think that's a bit WEIRD?

Azra: Did you plan this?

Plan this? Cassie's stomach curled. She knew Azra was angry, but that didn't feel fair. But there was no point saying that.

Cassie: I'm so sorry Azra. You know what I'm like! I'd gone and forgotten non-uniform day. But I promise you Fern didn't know anything about it. All my fault!!!!!!

Azra: **Fine. I believe you. But this is serious, Cassie. We look totally stupid in that photo. We had better make sure we win this thing now.**

Cassie gulped. She decided not to point out that there were over two hundred people in year seven who all wanted to redesign the uniform.

Cassie: **That would be so great! xx**

The entrance door opened and one of Cassie's neighbours – Mrs Khalid and her grandson – walked inside. He was lugging a rucksack of textbooks, a sports bag and a cello. Mrs Khalid was wearing a moss-green poncho. In the slants of autumn light from the windows, it looked as if Mrs Khalid had scooped up the floor of an enchanted forest and thrown it around her shoulders.

Cassie wanted to say she loved it and how the style reminded her of a 1930s' cape she'd seen in a fashion history video. But she stopped herself. Whenever anyone complimented Mrs Khalid's knitwear – and it was truly beautiful – Mrs Khalid would go on about this group she went to called the KnitWits, and she'd reel off the incredible things they made, and say how clever and creative they all were. Mrs Khalid's personal knitwear was very high end, but Cassie was not in the mood for a rundown of woolly creations by old people.

She tried to smile. 'Hiya!'

Mrs Khalid gave Cassie an understanding smile. 'Forgotten your key again?'

'No.' Cassie shook her head. 'All good, thanks.' She shoved her phone into her pocket. It was still buzzing.

'You're welcome to come up to mine, until Emily or your parents get home.'

'Thanks, but it's alright. Mum's home. I'm just having a little sit down.'

And a little breakdown.

The boy accidentally knocked Cassie's shoulder with his cello case as they went past. 'Sorry,' he said politely.

Cassie had never properly met Mrs Khalid's grandchildren. But if Cassie's mum was to be believed, they were in the top set for everything, musically gifted, Olympic standard at sports and such master chefs they could throw together a feast in minutes.

Mrs Khalid carried on up the stairs. 'If you change your mind, just come on up.'

'Will do, thanks.'

Cassie put her head in her hands. A montage of clips raced through her brain, like a film: *Cassie Coltsfoot and the Shacket from Hell*; Azra's shocked face when she realized why Cassie had hidden her clothes all day; the laughter when everyone saw her school uniform; Fern's confusion when Cassie left without even speaking to her.

She leant her back against the wall, which was covered from floor to ceiling in original Edwardian tiles – a remnant of when the building had been a fire station, back in the early twentieth century.

The building's firefighting days were long gone

but the place still felt reassuringly solid and safe. Occasionally there had been friends who had come over and gone on about how tiny their flat was. People wondered how she could live in a place that had space-saving fold-out beds, and dining table and chairs that slotted into the alcove like in a doll's house. Someone's mum had thought it was so cute she wondered if it was an Airbnb.

But Cassie loved everything about her home. She loved the classic fire station doors, and the pole that ran from outside the Coltsfoots' front door (that she and Emily slid down and Emily could climb up, even in her wellies) up to the writing carved above the hallway. *Ready? Aye, ready!* Emily had started a sort of a joke years ago that she and Cassie had to say those words every time they went past, to bring them luck. The routine was so familiar that Cassie muttered the words without thinking. But suddenly, tears sprang up in her eyes. Ready? *No, not ready.* Cassie hadn't been at all prepared for what today had thrown at her.

She heard a door open. Barry Allerton, who lived on the ground floor, appeared with his watering can.

Oh flip. She got to her feet. Barry was OK to a point, but that point was reached pretty quickly. Especially when Barry started reciting all the botanical names for the pots of flowers he looked after around the fire station flats.

Cassie ran up the stairs. 'The friendship plant is looking great!' she said, as she shoved her key into the lock.

'*Pilea involucrata* to you!' said Barry.

Cassie dropped her bag on the hallway floor and went to flop down on the sofa.

'You will not believe the day I've—'

'Thank goodness you're back!' said her mum. 'I need some help. ASAP.' She had a pole leant against the back wall, and coils of rope on the floor. 'Part of the raft came undone in a work session this morning. Not when we were crossing the river, by the way!'

Oh no. Cassie sighed inwardly. Mum's hair had stringy

bits of what looked like river weeds in it. She was still in her wetsuit, with a cardi thrown on top. It was all she needed. *Mum in Bear Grylls mode.* Cassie shut her eyes for a moment.

Her parents ran a survival skills adventure company. They took people hiking in Snowdonia, across the river on rafts, and taught them to make basic shelters in the forest. Cassie's dad was called Adrian and her mum Caitlyn. The company was called: *Adrenalyn!* But no one ever got it and they had to spell it out to people all the time.

'I need to reattach everything, and my hands are still freezing.' Mum rubbed them together. 'Grab this!' She picked up some rope and threw it to Cassie.

'Why?' said Cassie, catching it.

'I need you to do a clove hitch knot and get it back on the pole.'

'Can't I put the kettle on first?'

'Not until this is done.' Mum pushed a strand of hair out of her eyes. 'When it comes to survival, Cassandra, you can't just brew up whenever you want!'

'I know that!'

Mum tutted. 'The whole raft would fall to pieces while you're fatting about with a teapot.'

'My mistake.' Cassie looked around her. 'Didn't realize we were on the high seas.'

'Very funny.' Mum was folding a groundsheet. 'I don't have many life tips—'

'You do though.'

'But taking care of your kit is one of the first rules of—'

Cassie's phone buzzed on the side table.

'Ignore that,' said Mum.

'I can't.' Cassie shook her head. 'There's been a bit of a . . .' She went to grab her phone and her hands froze mid-air as her dad rolled over, noisily, pulling the duvet across himself. He was asleep on the platform bed, which stuck out from the wall like a large shelf above Mum's desk.

Cassie was used to this. The flat they lived in – which

had been Mum's before she and Dad had got together – only had two bedrooms. So, Cassie had one, Emily the other and their parents slept in the living room on the platform bed – which was where Dad often had a nap in the afternoons. Cassie tiptoed closer. The duvet was tucked under his chin, he had military camouflage face paint on and his feet were sticking out of the end of the bed. He looked like one of those living installations you see in art galleries.

Mum mouthed, 'How about you put the kettle on?'

'Not until we hit dry land!'

Mum laughed. 'The first rule of survival is to keep alert and adapt to the situation.'

Cassie went into the kitchen, stuck some crumpets in the toaster for herself and scooped caramel-flavoured tea into a pot, and got two mugs out.

'By the way, I heard from Mr Johnson,' said Mum, as she came into the kitchen.

'Mr Johnson?'

'Your form tutor!' Mum brushed the hair from her

face. 'Surely you remember him. You probably saw him less than an hour ago.'

Cassie's face flushed. 'You spoke to Mr Jackson?'

Mum laughed. 'No. It was only a message sent to everyone! Something about a new uniform design, but how parents and carers weren't to worry about having to buy a whole new outfit as it would take time to be introduced. But there was a link to the school social media and a photo of you in a Fashion Dream Team—'

Cassie's mind started racing. 'Did you get back to him?'

'Sorry.' Mum put her hand on Cassie's shoulder. 'I've been busy, but if you want me to reply, I—'

'Say I've broken my leg or something—'

Mum stared. 'Broken your leg! Why would I say that you'd broken your—'

'So I don't have to go into school on Monday.'

Mum's eyebrows knitted together 'What's going on?'

Cassie almost fell against the worktop in relief. At last, a chance to vent. She took a bite of crumpet to steady herself. If she didn't let go of some of this emotion, she might implode.

'Today's been the worst day of my life.'

Mum looked at Cassie's legs. 'You've not got another ladder in your tights? We went through two pairs last week,' she smiled. 'I don't think I can take the trauma of how humiliating you found it when—'

'Mum!' Cassie felt the tension of the day rising in her again. 'Just because I haven't had a free-fall parachuting accident doesn't mean I haven't had a bad day.'

Mum thinks I overreact, thought Cassie, and maybe she did get upset at stuff that wouldn't bother her mum or dad. Or Emily. But not this time. What happened today had changed everything.

Mum's phone rang. 'Oh, hello Mrs Khalid . . .'

Cassie slammed her plate down. One of the crumpets bounced off it and left a buttery smear on the worktop. As she grabbed a cloth and wiped it up, she heard her mum agreeing to pop round and fix Mrs Khalid's leaky tap. By the time Cassie had squeezed the cloth out,

Mum already had a spanner in her hand.

Mum pulled an apologetic face. 'Sorry Cassie, I've got to go to flat four.'

'Do you really have to go? Can't her grandson fix it?'

'Cassie! He's only eleven!' Mum was tapping the spanner on the worktop. 'Anyway, Mrs Khalid is a gem. Remember when she let you try on her old vintage clothes from the 1960s and 1970s?'

Cassie felt terrible. She didn't want Mrs Khalid to have water all over her kitchen. It was just that she *really* needed to talk to her mum right now.

'OK.' Mum put her hand on Cassie's shoulder. 'I've made those filo parcels that you like for dinner. Can you throw together a salad, and we'll catch up when I'm back?'

'Sure.'

Cassie's throat went tight. Her mum climbed breathtaking peaks, knew *High School Musical* off by heart, and made the best garlicky pasta in the world. And if Cassie ever did fall off a raft, she knew it would be her mum who would save her. But she was no one's idea of a good listener.

Cassie pulled out a cucumber from the fridge and dumped it on the chopping board. The kitchen was so tiny that this manoeuvre only involved a 180-degree turn. From here she could reach to the windowsill, where she grabbed a handful of tomatoes.

'Promise I'll only be a few minutes.' Mum rubbed a stain on her wetsuit with a dishcloth. She laughed. 'Good job *I'm* not in the Fashion Dream Team.'

A few minutes turned into seventy-five – not that Mum apologized when she finally turned up. She just sat down to dinner, and when Emily made the mistake of asking Mum about her day, Mum gave a deeply boring rundown of everything from the broken raft to the plumbing victory. The story took them all the way from the first bite of filo pastry to the end of the washing up. As soon as the last fork was thrown into the cutlery drawer, Cassie went off to her room.

She checked her phone: all quiet on the Azra front. But she could feel her brain about to spiral off again. To distract herself, Cassie did her favourite calm-down technique – she gave herself a tour of her own bedroom.

Going into Cassie's bedroom was like stepping into a wardrobe. Everywhere there were clothes. A flowy white dress, a blouse with balloon sleeves, pink and gold tee-shirts, a vest with ruffles and a cute denim skirt hung from hooks on the walls as if they were pictures. Her twenties' dress was suspended above the end of her bed, dangling on a wire from the ceiling like an otherworldly vision.

'Breathtaking!' Cassie said aloud, as if she were starting the tour. 'Note the simplicity of the shape, contrasting with the bejewelled neckline . . .' She twisted the wire to make the dress spin. The golden beads sparkled and shone as they caught the light, making the entire room shimmer.

It was a small room with a high ceiling so it actually looked like a walk-in cupboard.

Her jumpers and a pair of jeans were folded on top of a pile of books in the corner, shoes were lined up on the windowsill, underwear and tights were in a box under the bed. And belts, scarves and a feather boa (which she'd had since she was little) were draped over the chair. She picked it up now and wrapped it around her neck, the fake feathers tickling her.

'Fabulously over the top, and around since the nineteenth century . . . a feather boa is party dressing at its best!' said Cassie. She smiled, remembering a photo on the fridge: she was about five, wearing the feather boa on the swings in the park. 'Though I say, wear them anywhere!'

The same could be said for the 1960s' mini skirt that was hanging on the back of the door. It had belonged to Cassie's gran, who had paired it with boots while working in a seaside cafe. It had been revived in the nineties, when Cassie's mum had worn it over leggings, and now it was one of Cassie's most coveted pieces. She'd drawn a little butterfly in fabric paint to cover up a tiny stain on the pocket and wore it with bare legs and trainers.

Cassie traced her finger over the needlework. 'Whether it's the colour, the slightly itchy inside hem, or the way it moves when you dance, it's full of memories!'

She wandered over to her desk. There were strings of beads strewn across the top, along with some mismatched retro earrings. Behind them, there was a mirror decorated with fairy lights. Cassie switched them on. They created a cosy, glamorous vibe, like a dressing room in a theatre.

Next, she got into her bed shorts, a tee, and an old check shirt that had belonged to her grandpa and lay back against the cushions on her bed. She swiped her phone and clicked on one of her favourite fashion history creators.

There was a new post: a video about berets. It whizzed through how the hat was often worn by peasants back in the 1400s, right through to how it became a symbol of revolutionaries in the 1960s and the fashion statement of the 2020s.

Berets were chic, thought Cassie. *Plus, super practical. They suited everyone and they were ideal for covering up a bad hair day.* Her mind threw up an image of the school berets worn at Pipson High decades ago. Who had abolished the beret? What a mistake!

Her stomach clenched. What was she going to do about designing a new uniform? She couldn't get her head around the idea of wearing anything else. But if she was going to stay best friends with Azra, she was going to have to try. Azra was counting on her.

And then there was Fern. Cassie smiled. Fern would probably be into berets. She would like their whole revolutionary vibe. And if they customized it, Azra would love it too. Especially if it was covered with purple butterflies. Maybe they could be the girls who could bring back the beret . . .

There was a knock on her door. 'Can we come in?' Without waiting for an answer, both her parents came into the bedroom.

'We've got a bit of news,' Dad smiled. He brushed past a velvet jacket, which was looped over the curtain rail. It used to belong to Cassie's aunt, and Cassie thought it looked a bit like an Edwardian opera cloak. (Though she'd never been to the opera and had only ever worn it as a dressing gown.)

'You've sold Adrenalyn for a million pounds?' Cassie did a double thumbs up. 'I can leave school and Emily and I don't need GCSEs because you're going to give us all the money!'

'Good one,' said Dad.

He and Mum were wearing their branded Adrenalyn all-weather pyjamas. Even the sight of those pyjamas made Cassie feel sad. Her parents had excitedly put in a bulk order for hundreds, but only eight pairs had sold so far. As usual, they insisted on looking at the positive side ('How many people are lucky enough to have a lifetime's supply of pyjamas?'). Even so, Cassie wished people would just buy the things.

'In a way, it's better than that!' Mum sat on the bed.

She picked up a pair of Cassie's joggers and hugged them as if they were a cushion.

'Wow, I could use some good news today.' Cassie pretended to look excited.

Dad smiled, encouragingly. 'You know Mum and I have to work tomorrow? That we're taking a group up Yr Wyddfa, and Em will be out all day practising her climbing?'

'Sorry we have to work,' said Mum. 'But we can't turn down this booking . . .'

'Honestly, I'll be fine.' Cassie played it cool. A whole day alone in the flat! She couldn't wait. Hot chocolate and crumpets in bed with the latest journal from the *Costume Society*. Long soak in the bath. Music on while she customized her jeans . . .

Dad put his hand on her arm. 'Em's told us about what a hard day you've had.'

'And although it was probably not as bad as you think . . .' said Mum.

'We don't want you stuck on your own,' said Dad.

Cassie didn't like the way this was going. No way was she hiking up a mountain with them. 'I'm fine. I've got loads to do.'

Mum pointed at the logo on her PJs. The fabric was navy, and there was a tiny, green, snow-capped tent sewn on the pocket, and the words: Adrenalyn: *the rush of adventure, every day!*

'Exactly that!' said Cassie. 'Today has been pretty wild, so tomorrow I need to recover. Here, at base camp . . .'

Dad shook his head. 'What you need is a treat!'

'Thanks – but I've got this!'

Mum and Dad's idea of a treat was to sleep outdoors in a freezing-cold bivvy bag.

'So, we thought,' said Dad, with a smile, 'what does Cassie love to do? And where might she—'

Mum cut in. 'You're off to the KnitWits! It's the local crafting group in the community centre—'

Cassie jumped off the bed. 'I know what it is, Mum!' Her stomach flipped over. 'Mrs Khalid mentions it constantly. And there's no way I'm going. NO. WAY.'

'Mrs Khalid says it's wonderful. A real community,' Mum said, briskly.

The KnitWits! It sounded like a show for toddlers. Cassie pictured a row of knitted socks with googly eyes and pretend woolly hair singing a stupid song about being together.

'When she heard you'd be alone all day, she offered to take you with her.'

'Thanks a lot, Mum, you went and told a neighbour I have no friends.' Cassie ran her fingers through her hair in disbelief. 'And now I have to hang out with random old people.'

'Not just olds!' said Dad, cheerfully. 'One of Mrs Khalid's granddaughters goes apparently.'

It was sounding worse by the minute.

'Can't you make Emily go?' Cassie said, her voice breaking. 'She could use it as one of her volunteer hours for her Duke of Edinburgh Award.'

'Cassie!' Mum looked super annoyed. 'It's not about volunteering. Unless, of course, you count Mrs Khalid, who is giving her time to you. Voluntarily.'

Cassie felt bad. 'I know that. Sorry, I just meant . . .'

'I'm sorry you're not keen,' said Dad, sounding disappointed. 'We thought you'd like the idea. Look at it this way, though, they're very old, so they're practically living history, and they're into making their own clothes. And you love fashion history.' He looked around at all the clothes hanging on the walls. 'So, who knows, Cas? It could be an amazing day!'

Chapter 3

Cassie pushed open the door. She hadn't been in the community centre since a birthday party when she was six and Lia Hart, from her primary school, had been sick all over the bouncy castle.

Cassie smoothed down her top. She was wearing her sixties' mini skirt, with a white tee, trainers and a grey wrap cardigan that wouldn't have been out of place in a period drama from the forties.

She walked down the corridor, telling herself that however much of a cringefest the KnitWits was, there was no way it could be worse than the Assembly disaster.

Cassie had woken up to a fresh set of messages:

Azra is online . . .

Azra: Have you seen the likes on the photo of us on the Year 7 group chat?

Azra: I don't think I really got it before. But people seem to love Fern! They say she's got a cute, relatable boho look. And I don't like it personally but that homemade uniform means Fern is fashion famous!!!!!!

Azra: You awake????

Azra: This is great for us! Everyone already likes how Fern cares about fashion. Who knew?!!!!! I'm suddenly thinking that with Fern on our team, we might have a shot at winning the competition.

Azra: We need to get designing though. Having Fern means we might win because people like her, but there's no way I want to wear a uniform by her. I'm not being mean because it's not like I can sew myself either but (Have you seen the wonky pleats on her skirt???).

Cassie is online . . .

Cassie: I'm awake. That's great Az! I'll get designing. xxx

Azra: Sorry, and by uniform fashion designing, I mean . . . normal stuff, Cassie. We don't want historical stuff and we don't want something sooooo bad it needs to be covered up with a shacket!!!!!!!! Hahaha!

Cassie: Haha! Think the rules said it had to be a team effort so we should get Fern on it too? Like you said, her style is super popular (unlike mine!!!) xxxx

Azra: Let's get together on our own first. My mum says you can come over here. I've got pink wafer biscuits . . .

Cassie sighed. Azra was being nice. But Azra also knew Cassie preferred Jammie Dodgers. She wished Azra didn't think they were babyish and that it was Azra's responsibility to get her into a better biscuit.

Cassie: Thanks! I can't come today. Be great to do it soon tho xxx

Azra: Why? What are you doing?

Cassie switched her phone off before Azra could reply.

She was outside a door now, which had a sign written in calligraphy, which said: *Welcome to the KnitWits.*

'What is it?' said a man in a deep, velvety-rich, authoritative tone. He had a large, square-ish face lined with wrinkles.

Cassie looked into the room.

She suddenly felt a sparkle of excitement. It didn't *look* like a community knitting group. There were tables set up with sewing machines and a woman with a mouthful of pins was trying a balloon sleeve on another woman. Others were busy cutting out fabric. There was a table piled with rolls of cloth, balls of squishy wool and silky ribbons flowing like water over the edge of an infinity pool.

But there was no sign of Mrs Khalid.

The man gave Cassie a quizzical stare.

She gulped. 'I just wondered if—'

'Beginners' Mandarin is next door.' He stood up and pointed. There was a silvery robe hanging around his shoulders. The man, who looked as old and ragged as Gandalf, seemed to be knitting the robe at the same time as wearing it. Cassie tried not to stare. *Talk about Lord of the Rings energy.*

'Thanks, but—'

There was a long loop of wool, from his hand to his elbow, which he pulled through to form a stitch. 'Or if you want the webcomic workshop, it's down the corridor on the left,' said the man, in his powerful, throaty voice, as if he was giving directions to Mordor.

'What a lot of classes,' said a younger man, in a friendly Slovakian accent. He was younger, with a massive floppy fringe of dark hair and zippy jeans. He was sewing a midnight-blue, sequined, long skirt. He'd knitted an over layer and swathed the fabric in pearls and floral corsages. He stood up and shook it out.

Cassie's mouth dropped open. It was as if he was throwing stars and petals into the night sky. 'Wow!' she breathed.

'In or out?' The older man pointed towards the door.

Before Cassie could say anything else, Mrs Khalid appeared. 'There you are, Cassie! Come on in.' She was holding balls of wool in one hand, and a mug of tea in the other. Mrs Khalid pointed to a chair and then she shouted back into the kitchen. 'Samira! Come and meet Cassie.'

A girl came out of the kitchen, with big wavy hair, a Taylor Swift knit, dramatic sweeps of eyeliner, and reams of sequined material thrown around her shoulders. The fabric wafted in the breeze from the open window, like a cloud of sparkly dry ice. Cassie's mouth dropped open.

It was Mira Lal.

Cassie threw herself down in the chair.

'Cassie, this is my granddaughter, Samira. Samira, Cassie is my friend and neighbour,' said Mrs Khalid, with a smile. 'OK. Let's get going.'

Cassie's heart raced. Wait until she told Azra! She mentally fired off a message:

> **Cassie: You know when I said I was helping out a neighbour? Well, you're NEVER going to believe who . . .**

Mrs Khalid picked up a bag with needles in various sizes. Her arms jangled with gold bangles. She looked up. 'Maybe you know each other from school?'

Cassie was about to say yes. That they'd actually talked yesterday. But that even if they hadn't she would still have known who Mira was because *everyone* knew Mira Lal.

'No, we don't,' Mira said, flatly.

Oh.

'Well, you're meeting now,' said Mrs Khalid. She wound some wool around her needle. 'Do you know how to cast on?'

Cassie shook her head.

Mrs Khalid introduced Cassie to everyone, going around saying people's names. 'You've met Milo.' She pointed to the younger man with the midnight skirt. 'And Allan.' She nodded at the Gandalf lookalike. 'This is Leta and Serena . . .'

There were over a dozen people all in, waving and saying hello. Mrs Khalid told Cassie about everyone's clothes as she said their names. Everything was handmade. Serena was wearing a mini skirt in a tapestry-like fabric, which used to be a carpet bag, Leta's headscarf had once been a dress, Milo's patchwork sweatshirt had been made with pairs of old jeans, and Allan had unravelled some moth-eaten jumpers to make his robe.

By the time she'd finished, Mrs Khalid had already cast on thirteen stitches and knitted several rows. She passed the needles to Cassie. 'Your mum said you'd love to learn how to knit?'

Did she? That sounded like Mum, Cassie thought. One

of Mum's life tips was to never turn down the chance to learn a new skill. Cooking, chess or canoeing, it could save your life one day, according to Mum.

'Thanks, that would be great.'

'I'll teach you how to make the same scarf Samira is making.'

Cassie did a sideways look at Mira. She was doing big loops with her fingers around big wooden needles. The wool was cobalt blue. 'It's amazing.'

'The scarf only uses the basic knit stitch,' Mrs Khalid said. 'It's done loosely and on big needles. Learning to knit just takes practice. Samira's very fast now but it took her time to get there.' She smiled.

'Thanks for that,' said Mira, with an eye roll.

'Huh!' Mrs Khalid made an amused noise. She picked up the shrug she had made. Along the hem Mrs Khalid was stitching tiny pink roses, the size of flowers on a doll's house. It elevated the piece to beyond gorgeous.

'Who taught you to be so good you helped knit your own sweater?' Mrs Khalid pointed at Mira's Taylor

Swift cardi.

'It's not genuine?' blurted Cassie. 'As in, I mean, it's not official merch?'

Mira smiled. 'Obviously not.'

'It's genuine KnitWits,' said Mrs Khalid, good-naturedly. 'Samira did the cuffs, and I did the sleeves and the back; Serena and Leta did the sides. We all did some stars, Milo sewed it all together.'

'A communal garment, if you like,' said Allan, pointedly. 'With all of us involved.'

'Oh yes, and Allan did the measurements, so we got it the exact fit Samira wanted.' Mrs Khalid explained how Allan was a professor of Maths at the university. 'He's an expert at calculating the patterns.'

'And doing Maths homework,' said Mira.

Mrs Khalid shot her look. 'Keep the loops straight.'

'Talking of showstoppers,' said a woman called Leta, pleasantly, 'where's the showstopper shacket this week, Mira?' Leta was in her sixties, with a brightly patterned shift dress, a cardigan and a silver locket around her neck. She explained to Cassie how Samira had an eye-catching top in red and yellow, which was a contrast to Samira's usual outfits. 'Joyous colour combination! We've all been admiring it for weeks.'

Mira didn't look up from her knitting.

'Yes, where is it?' said Mrs Khalid. 'That was your birthday present. Why aren't you wearing it?'

There was a moment of silence.

'I just thought I'd give it a break today because a girl in year seven wore the same thing during Assembly,' said Mira, finally.

'So?' said Mrs Khalid, sharply. 'It's not like we made it here, it's not unique to you.'

Cassie felt a big kick of embarrassment. Mrs Khalid must have known it was her. She'd seen her crying on the stairs in Emily's shacket. Cassie nervously played with her wool.

'And that's it?' said Leta, as she knitted a sleeve. 'A younger girl wore the same thing as you and now . . .' She looked confused. 'Sorry, am I missing something?'

Mira fiddled with her serpent bangle. 'It wasn't her fault,' she said slowly, as she twisted it around. She didn't meet Cassie's eyes. 'But the girl had what you could call . . . a fashion disaster . . . not that *I* would call it that,' she said quickly. She flushed. 'But it's why no one thinks the top is cool any more.'

OMG, Cassie thought, *Mira can't even wear her favourite birthday shacket because of what I did*. Tears sprang into her eyes. Emily hadn't said anything about it, but she must have felt the same way.

She'd literally ended the shacket trend. Her stomach flipped. *I'm the opposite of fashion fearless.*

'You should be feeling sorry for that girl and not for your reputation,' said Mrs Khalid sharply. 'And you shouldn't stop wearing that shacket.'

Mira shook her head, like she was annoyed with herself. 'I just thought I'd leave it at home today, that's all.'

Mrs Khalid shifted her chair next to Cassie. 'Knitting,' she said, in a soft, comforting way. 'Simple knitting.

Distracts the brain like nothing else.' She showed Cassie how to insert the right-hand needle into the front loop of the first stitch, from left to right. 'Let's give it a go, shall we?'

Cassie blinked back her tears. She focused on the wool. She did exactly what she was told.

'Beautiful!' said Mrs Khalid a few minutes later. 'You're a natural.'

Cassie did a half smile. Probably Mrs Khalid was just being nice. Once she got the first few rows done, she'd thank everyone, run home, and dive under the duvet. Then she'd work out how to move schools before Monday.

Two hours later, and Cassie felt totally different.

Who knew knitting was such a major buzz? Cassie's mood had shot skywards. Repetitive and rhythmic, the click of the needles and the sight of the rows appearing was relaxing yet exhilarating. And she'd had to focus so hard that it blocked obsessive thoughts. Cassie was practically singing to herself. *I want to knit for ever*, she thought.

Her mind raced. Once she got really good, maybe she could make a bag for Emily? Her sister was always saying she needed one to put her chalk in for dusting her hands when she was climbing. And . . . hats! Cosy and comforting, woolly beanies would be ideal for her parents when they were at work. Cassie's heart did a little skip. Maybe she could even do a little Adrenalyn logo on them?

She pictured herself in an offbeat woollen top, a bag of yarn slung over her shoulders, a pair of needles worn in her hair. She'd be known as Knitting Girl. People would ask her how she got the perfect knit for every 'fit. She smiled. *What this? I made it myself . . .*

After a while, Mrs Khalid taught Cassie to cast off. The wool was chunky and there were only a few stitches across, so it hadn't taken long. The last stitch slipped off the needles and Cassie felt a whoosh of excitement as she tied the knot. Even Mira joined in with the little clap.

'Thank you!'

Cassie held it up. She loved everything about it. The wool was silky as a periwinkle, the loops chaotic but somehow perfect. She wrapped it around her head, with a twist in the middle, 1940s' style. The blue made Cassie's hair shine like conkers against an evening sky.

Leta put down her knitted sleeve. 'Superb!'

Milo did a double thumbs up. 'It took me ages to get that good.'

Allan had his hand on his chunky knitting needle, like it was a staff. 'Thirteen stitches on a row and it took you just over two hours. Can you check the number of rows and tell me how many stitches you did per minute?'

Cassie went red. She hated doing those sort of Maths problems.

'Don't feel the pressure to answer,' said Mira. 'I never do.'

'Approximate is fine,' said Allan. 'If that helps.'

'Your first project!' said Mrs Khalid. 'It looks fantastic.' She passed Cassie a packet of Jammie Dodgers and sent

Mira to put the kettle on again.

A woman called Serena was stitching a velvet bodice, edged with a gleaming blue ribbon and a low square back. It reminded Cassie of a painting she'd seen in her fashion history book: *The Blue Dress*, Auguste Toulmouche, 1872.

Serena saw Cassie staring. She smiled and tossed her lobbed hair. 'You like it?'

'I love it,' Cassie breathed. 'It looks like a beautiful painting come to life.'

Mira handed out the mugs of tea.

'Thanks, Mira,' said Allan, taking one. 'From what I can see, the approximate answer is 1.6, if anyone was interested.'

Serena explained how the velvet fabric had come from an old pair of hot pants. 'My clubbing days in Paris . . .'

Mira ran her fingers down the velvet. 'And they're French? Even cooler!'

'Actually, they used to belong to my cousin and she's from Manchester,' said Serena, with a laugh. 'But I did wear them in Paris, honestly. Along with waistcoats that I got from thrift shops. What?' she looked at Mira. 'They were very in at the time!'

Leta laughed. 'I remember! I used to wear waistcoats over dresses. I had this amazing fabric that I got in Ghana.' She described the pattern and how she'd even sewn on hand-painted buttons.

'Wow! Do you still have it? That sounds incredible,' said Cassie.

Leta shook her head. 'I passed it on to my niece. She still wears it with jeans and a tee.'

'That's quite the endorsement,' said Mrs Khalid. She smiled at Cassie. 'Leta's niece is a student at Art school.'

'You should set up your own fashion label,' said Cassie. 'Honestly, you could totally sell this stuff!'

Serena nodded. 'Maybe we should. We could make things together.'

'And they'd go for loads,' said Cassie.

'Seriously,' said Mira. 'Don't encourage them.'

Too late, thought Cassie. Serena was scrolling her

phone and showing everyone how Mira's cardigan was going for a fortune. Allan was zooming in on the different versions – black, purple, white, red, green – and claiming the KnitWits version was better made. 'At those prices, I should give up my job and knit full time!'

A minute later they seemed to have decided to send Mira's cardi to Taylor Swift. As soon as she saw it, apparently, Taylor would be blown away by their skills and ask them to supply all her official knitwear.

'We'll be known as Taylor's Tailors! Get it?' said Milo. He was doing the final stitches on the waistband of the skirt. It was on his lap, looking super frothy next to his jeans and workman's boots.

'Yes, right!' Mira laughed. 'She'll be, "Oh KnitWits, you're so incredible, I want to commission you to make me a sensational dress and, tell you what, I'll wear it on my next album cover."'

Cassie caught Mira's eye. They both laughed. *Phew.*

Serena rolled her eyes. 'OK, maybe we're getting carried away . . .'

'But talking of sensational outfits . . .' Allan's face clouded over. 'Reminds me of the competition . . .'

Mira buried her face in her scarf. 'Here we go. For the zillionth time, my GCSEs start in 257 days, and I need to revise. There is no way I'm being your model for the competition.'

Model? Cassie's heart began to beat faster. *Competition?*

'Don't worry.' Mrs Khalid put her hand on Mira's arm. 'She's in year eleven, Allan, she has homework to do.'

Leta explained to Cassie that there was a competition called *CommunKnitty*, which the group had considered entering. Each group had to produce a collaborative piece – a dress or a jumpsuit, say – to show what can be achieved when communities come together. And if possible, it had to be made from fabric that people already had, so it was a zero-cost, low-impact project.

'The problem is,' Serena ran her fingers through her hair, 'we have to apply by midnight tonight,' she said.

'You need a dress by midnight?' Cassie's heart sank.

Even for the KnitWits that was a big ask.

'No.' Allan stuck his needle into his robe. 'We just need to *register* by midnight. We then have around a fortnight to produce a garment.'

Cassie shifted in her seat. 'And model it?'

'The competition is about real clothes made by real people,' said Serena. 'The model is more of a muse, really, a creative person who has worked on the garment and can then show it off because they love it.' She snipped a thread from the sleeve she was sewing. She'd sewn a tiny pearl button on the cuff.

Cassie felt sparkles of excitement. 'So, they'd get to wear something you've made?'

'Of course! It would be made just for them,' said Serena.

Dress fittings! Sweeps of satin! Sleeves puffed to exactly the right shape. An entire outfit made just for her. Cassie imagined herself arms outstretched and twirling in a skirt as magical as midnight.

There was a cough. She looked up. Mira shot her a

look that said *don't even think about getting involved*.

Mrs Khalid popped her needles back into her bag. 'We've not done a collaboration since Samira's cardigan, so we're miles behind.'

'We've got to be realistic.' Milo dunked a biscuit in his tea, and then began to collect everyone's mugs.

'We wouldn't do ourselves justice,' said Leta. 'Not if we rushed it.'

Everyone began to talk about how busy they were at work, or at home, and how they had extra things on that meant they just couldn't give it enough time.

'We've still got a fortnight to produce a garment.' Allan was going on like a stuck needle. 'We're always saying we want new members, and younger people to join and learn skills,' he said. He was pacing around the chairs. 'The competition is basically free marketing . . .'

People were packing away. Someone scooped up the ribbons and fabric into a box and put it in a cupboard. Most of them were avoiding Allan's eyes. Serena and Leta were slowly putting on their coats but looked reluctant to leave. Milo put his hand on Allan's back. 'This has to be a group decision. We've not got the numbers.'

Mrs Khalid gave a friendly shrug of her shoulders. 'I don't think we can pull it off in time. Sorry, Allan. Maybe next year?'

'This competition? It's an absolute NO,' said Mira, as they left the hall. 'Don't encourage them, I mean it.'

They'd said goodbye to the others. Mrs Khalid needed to swing by the supermarket, so Mira was getting the bus and Cassie was walking back home.

Cassie could feel her good mood evaporating. 'You don't think they'll win? But they're so talented.' Cassie pulled her cardigan around her. 'And you don't have to be the model. I know you want to concentrate on your GCSEs.'

'Sure!' Mira slapped her palm against her forehead. 'That was an excuse, Cassie. My GCSEs are ages away. And I only care about my Art grade anyway . . .'

'What then?'

'It's too high risk because of school, of course.' Mira looked frustrated. 'What if someone finds out about the competition? You heard Allan. He wants to use the publicity as marketing for the group! Think about it, Cassie. Everyone will know that I go to the KnitWits!'

'What's so bad about that?' Cassie took a breath. To be fair, Mira had a point. Only last night, Cassie had been appalled at the thought of going to the KnitWits.

'Look, I love the KnitWits, mainly because I come here to spend time with my nani, and I genuinely love knitting—'

'So do I now!' Cassie kicked some leaves. 'And I've only done a headband. With lots of help, obviously.'

MIra laughed. 'Knitting, as they say, brings you life.'

She told Cassie about how she'd been going to the KnitWits since she was about eight or nine and all the things she'd made: from pencil cases to scrunchies to scarves and sleeves of cardigans.

'They're so talented,' said Mira. 'Have you seen that guitar strap that my friend Bella wears every day?'

'Yes! It's so cool!'

'Leta showed me how to crochet it out of ripped-up pairs of jeans made into yarn. I gave it to Bella for her birthday.'

'So, Bella thinks the KnitWits are cool?'

Mira's face clouded over. '*No one* thinks the KnitWits are cool, Cassie.' She looked guilty. 'Bella thinks I got that strap from Etsy.'

They didn't talk for a few minutes. They paced along towards the bus stop. Finally, Mira said, 'That's partly why I can't risk them being in the competition. Someone will hear about it and then trace that back to me. And if they knew the truth—'

'I'm not going to say anything!'

'OK.' Mira's face softened. 'It's not really that I don't want people to laugh at me. Well, it's not only that. I truly love the KnitWits, and I don't want everyone at school to laugh at *them* . . .'

'I get it. I promise.'

'And if you want my advice,' said Mira, in a way that

made it seem like it was more of a demand than an idea, 'you won't tell anyone at school that you are part of the group either.'

Part of the group! Mira Lal says I'm part of the group. 'I won't!' Cassie touched her knitted headband. This was the best day ever. No way was she going to mess this up. 'So, we're Secret KnitWits?'

Mira laughed. 'You're a KnitWit alright.'

Chapter 4

Ms Ginty: **To all year sevens**

It's Monday! Who put on their uniform today knowing they could design something better? There are just over two weeks for the project (think of it as fashion fortnight!) so start dreaming up an outfit that will take Pipson High to the next level. Uniform Fashion Designers go!

Ms Ginty posted the uniform project rules

Azra: **If you get the early bus come to the canteen! I'm going to find out what people actually want for their uniform so we can design it, and WIN!**

Azra posted a photo of a lilac notebook

> **Azra:** Bringing in my favourite sparkly notebook! Perfect for notes about fashion so we can design the perfect uniform!!!!!

> **Cassie @ Azra:** Sounds great x

> **Fern:** Got a fishy idea Cassie! Think we can make a real difference with this project. Shall we meet with Azra after school?

> **Cassie @ Fern:** See you there x

'Did you get that thing surgically attached?' said Emily. She pointed to Cassie's headband.

'What?'

'Did the KnitWits actually stitch it to your hair? Because you've not taken it off since you got home on Saturday, having found your calling,' Emily clasped her hands to her chest, 'and become one of the worldwide network of knitters—'

'Actually, they call it a knitwork.' Cassie grinned. Just touching the loopy wool gave her a whoosh of confidence. She held her phone out and took another selfie. She couldn't decide which filter the headband looked best with. Not that it needed a filter. The colour was perfect as it was.

Mrs Khalid had popped around yesterday to give Cassie some spare knitting needles, and a crochet hook and some wool so she could start her own project to work on at the KnitWits.

'Knitting is so cool, Em.'

'So you said!' Emily put a packed lunch into each of their bags and picked up her red cap and pulled it on. 'It's cold out there! Are you wearing your coat today?'

Cassie pulled a face. 'Azra said when you're at high school you have to go coatless for the sake of fashion.'

'I thought you said people like Holly have a massive coat?'

'Yes but she never wears it.'

Emily rolled her eyes. 'How about knitted coats?'

'Well—'

'Ha! Got you there,' laughed Emily.

'I can't tell Azra about the KnitWits, though, can I? It's so annoying, Em! I've had the best weekend I've had in ages and now—'

'Do you hear that?' said Dad, coming into the hallway. He was talking to Mum, who was in the sitting room, a slice of toast in one hand, and a stick of military face paint in the other. 'Best weekend in ages!' He looked pleased. 'Felt awful having to work all day Saturday, but I'm so glad you had a good way to spend your day.'

'And the rest of your life, apparently,' said Emily. She put a slick of strawberry lip gloss on. 'What with all the endless headband photos and the modelling—'

'Em!' Cassie shot her a warning look. 'I told you I wanted to be the model in *confidence*. Anyway, they're not even entering the competition in the first place.'

'Who's being a model?' said Mum, coming into the hallway.

'Sorry,' Emily mouthed.

Mum had a thick base layer of factor 50, followed by green concealer to imitate camouflage face paint.

'You,' said Emily. 'For a Halloween range.'

Cassie shot her a grateful smile.

Mum laughed. 'Trick or treat?' she said in a spooky voice. 'Actually this is camo for work.' A local firm had booked Adrenalyn for a team-building exercise.

Cassie suddenly felt a rush of nerves about school. 'I wish I could come with you and hide out along the river. I'm that desperate.'

'Everyone will have forgotten Assembly,' said Emily. 'And you said yourself that Azra was being OK now.'

'Hm,' said Cassie. She touched her headband. The best way to make everyone forget was to replace that image they had of her with a better one. Ideally one where she and Mira Lal were wearing matching knitwear.

Dad pulled on a utility belt. It had straps and hooks for Swiss army knives, pens and a pocket for Kendal mint cake. 'If you want to be a model, Cassie, you could wear this if you like. We're thinking of putting in an order and selling them on Adrenalyn courses. You could help with marketing—'

'Come on, Em, we'll be late.' Cassie grabbed her bag.

Dad picked up his phone. He pretended to take a photo of himself at a ridiculous angle. 'There you go!' said Dad, as if he was offering a major modelling contract. 'Your first job.'

'The belt's great, but I don't really want to be a model.' Cassie opened the front door. 'I was only joking.'

'Can I ask you what your favourite fashion trend is?'

When Cassie arrived at school, Azra was at the front of the queue in the canteen. And she'd embraced being a Uniform Fashion Designer with a passion. There was a purple butterfly clip at the back of Azra's hair, struggling to contain her mass of beautiful curls, and her shirt collar was standing up straight. Cassie peered closer. Had Azra done something with her eyelashes too?

While people were trying to buy toast and juice, Azra

was hopping about, throwing out questions and writing in her lilac notepad. She was getting people to tell her their favourite styles of jeans, and answer quick fire questions like:

'Frills or ribbons?'

'Belts or sashes?'

'Blazers or hoodies?'

As Cassie approached, she heard a girl in year ten say the key to her look was bedazzled crop tops; while her friend said she didn't go anywhere without an oversized tote bag.

'Getting lots of ideas?'

Azra's head whipped around. 'I love your headband! Yet another fashion surprise.' She put her palm to her forehead. 'I spent ages working on my uniform fashion designer look . . . and then you walk in with another new thing!'

'I love your look.' Cassie put her own collar up. 'There! We can look the same.'

Azra looked excited. 'Where's it from?'

'Where's what from?' *Help!* She should have known Azra would ask.

'The headband! You're right, Cassie. We should have a coordinated look.' Azra flushed. 'I may have said that before . . .' She flicked her hands and recovered herself. 'But we can now. If I buy the same headband as you—'

'You can't buy it—'

Azra's smile froze on her face. 'Oh no! Was it a limited edition or—'

Cassie went red. 'Because it's not for sale.'

'So how did you get it?'

'It was a . . . gift.'

'Who from?'

'The neighbour I said I was helping out on Saturday.' *Was that a lie?* wondered Cassie. She hoped it wasn't. Her stomach twisted. It *felt* like a lie. Technically, Mrs Khalid had given her the wool and there was no way she could have made it without her help. Cassie's mind spun forward. *At the weekend, I was taught to knit. Truly it was the greatest gift anyone could have given me.*

'Can you ask where they got it from?' Azra pushed a bit more. 'No one minds being asked. I just mean the shop . . .'

'Maybe! I think it was . . .' Cassie scrambled for an answer. 'A new brand . . .'

'Oh phew! I thought you were going to say vintage.'

Oh damn. I should have said vintage.

'Your neighbour's got great taste!' Azra perked up. 'She must be cool to know about new brands. What was the brand?'

'The brand?'

'Let me have a look.' Azra held her hand out.

Cassie shook her head. There was no way she'd think the headband was shop-bought if she saw it close up. Cassie had pulled the part with her mistakes in the stitches to the back of her head.

'I can't take it off because my hair's all caught up in it.' Cassie felt her cheeks get hot. 'But I think it's something like . . .' Her mind raced. What could she say? 'KW! I think that was it.'

'KW?' Azra smiled. 'I'll look out for it! And next time you see your neighbour ask where they sell KW stuff!' Azra looked at her notebook. 'Think we've got everything we need.'

'Hang on, did you say you were on Fern's team?' said the girl, who had white socks on over her black tights.

Azra looked a bit put out. 'Well, we're on each other's. It's the same team.'

'Have you seen the bows on her trainers?' said the girl.

That got a reaction from a few other girls in the canteen, who had seen them too. Cassie swiped her phone to see that Fern had posted a video clip of herself in the cloakroom threading her trainers with turquoise ribbons.

'OMG! Jane Austen vibes.' Cassie was excited. The bows-on-shoes look made her think of Regency fashion. 'What a cool idea! It could be part of the new uniform? Plus, roses! Roses on shoes are totally 1800s too!'

'Exactly! They're way out of date!' Azra was speaking

so loudly her fringe was flipping up and down.

Cassie tapped one of her feet, like she was beginning the steps of a formal dance. 'We could twist bows and roses onto everyone's shoes.' *And be like the Bennets off to the Netherfield Ball!*

Azra had her head in her hands.

The girl with the socks over tights looked confused. 'It's a new trend, actually. But I love how Fern's done a zero-waste version with ribbons she's saved from her birthday.'

Cassie smiled. 'That's really cool.'

Azra waved her notebook. 'Thanks for this, everyone! I've got some amazing ideas.'

'We'll be the judge of that,' said Holly, suddenly appearing beside them. She and Bea had almond milkshakes, and pin badges on their jumpers saying COORDINATORS.

'Look forward to seeing how you're going to mix fairy core with oversized totes,' said Bea, leaning over Azra's shoulder. 'Haha!'

Holly sucked hard on her milkshake. 'What Ginty is looking for is an outfit that takes us all to the next level and reminds us of the stars that we are. Like my lip gloss. I don't just put it on to make my lips shine; it's a little reminder to believe in myself.'

Cassie hid a smile. *And a little reminder for the rest of us that you've just got a new lip balm.*

'By the way,' added Bea, pushing her hair back. 'You don't wear big bags with fairy frills.'

'It's one or the other,' said Holly, authoritatively. 'Unless you're a fashion influencer, which by the way none of you are.'

As everyone headed off to the form room, Holly and Bea ran through their uniform style rules. Cassie tried to tune out of the conversation, but it was hard to ignore them. Holly was bellowing out the basics: ties worn wide; skirts rolled over at the waistband, shirts hanging loose. And Bea was echoing everything Holly said, and making it clear to everyone that they wanted an on-trend, sophisticated vibe. And Azra was frantically scribbling in her notebook, like she was being told the secret of how to win the competition.

After a minute or two of this, Holly started talking about what she called 'the jumper of dreams'. Cassie sighed. They may only have been at Pipson High for three weeks, but already everyone in 7B had been told about Holly's jumper a million times.

Faded and iconic (Holly's words) the jumper had been handed down to her from her cousin Ada. But according to Holly, it wasn't really a hand-me-down, it was more like a vintage family heirloom.

Cassie pretended to be checking her bag for her Spanish homework. She didn't want anyone to see what a wind-up she was finding Holly and Bea.

'You can't buy them like this!' Holly stroked the sleeve. 'It's almost too good to wear. The new ones that you lot wear are bright navy, thick and fluffy! You look like baby blue chicks. No one would EVER look at one of you and think you're in year eight.'

There was a slight groan from some of the others. Even Jules winced when Holly said that. They'd all heard how another year seven had asked Holly the way to the Music Rooms. Holly was convinced this was because she looked loads older than the others, and not because she was carrying her violin at the time.

'That was so exciting!' Bea high-fived Holly.

Cassie tried to block them out.

Cassie loved that 7B's form room was in the oldest part of the school. But it took ages to get there from the canteen. Which was a problem when Holly and Bea were waltzing ahead of the crowd, and Azra was stressing about every word they said.

The school was massive. Different blocks had been built over the years. New, shiny copper-and-glass buildings were stuck onto an old seventies block, which looked like a multistorey car park, and was a long walk from the original Victorian school, with its high ceilings, red bricks and ornate green tiles in the bathrooms.

Finally, they rounded the corner to the Art

department where 7B's form room was at the end of the corridor. Along with the others, Cassie weaved her way to her table between easels and sinks. She ducked under the washing line of GCSE artwork, which was strung across the room.

The project was 'Reflections', and Mira's piece was easily recognizable. She'd drawn a sewing machine, with her face reflected in all of the mirrored parts. It was really good. But Cassie felt nervous looking at it. She thought of Mira's intense expression when she said she couldn't mention the KnitWits.

Azra was nudging her. 'Colours!'

'What?' Cassie snapped back to focus.

'Haven't you been listening?' Azra looked worried. 'Everyone's talking about what colour the new uniform could be. I didn't even know we could change the colour! I didn't ask anyone in the canteen about colours, just styles . . .'

'I didn't know we could change it,' parroted Bea. She did her TV audience laugh. 'I want to design a whole new uniform but I didn't fink about colours.'

'If I was entering the competition instead of *coordinating* it, Azra, I'd be thinking big.' Holly did a little shimmy of her shoulders in her jumper. 'I wouldn't let anything stop me designing the uniform of my dreams.'

'I won't, I won't,' said Azra. She widened her eyes at Cassie.

'Not that blue's a problem for me.' Holly flicked her hair. 'I'm sooooo lucky the way it suits my hair colour!'

'Yeah,' said Bea. 'You suit it so much, Holly.'

A few of the other girls were wondering if they suited blue. Jules was saying her hair might suit it, because in Art, they'd learnt that orange was on the other side of the colour spectrum to blue. But even she wasn't sure.

Cassie felt her stomach clench. A flash of ultramarine velvet flew through her mind; a streak of cobalt blue balloon sleeves; a skirt as magical as midnight.

'Everyone suits blue! You just have to find your right shade. But anyway, our uniform is navy and that's basically a neutral.'

Holly's nose flared with annoyance. 'I think I know what suits me, thank you very much, Cassie.' She stared meaningfully at Cassie's knitted headband. 'Is that new? Where's it from?'

'Hard to say.' Cassie's stomach fizzed with panic.

'Holly needs more info!'

Azra looked like someone had stuck a STRESSED filter over her face. 'Didn't you say the brand was called KW?'

'KW?' Holly looked interested. She swiped her phone. 'Not getting any search results for KW headbands.'

'It's totally new!' said Azra. 'Cassie's cool neighbour knows all about it. Soon as we know anything more, we'll let you know.'

Cassie's face went red. 'It's an up-and-coming brand. Sort of secret, actually. The headband is a one-off piece of work . . . and I'm not even meant to talk about it.'

Azra stared at her. 'Your neighbour works in fashion?'

'No! God, no. Honestly, that's all I can say.'

'But it's a new brand?' said Bea.

Cassie could feel her heart beating in her ears. 'Sort of. But they're still . . . undiscovered.'

Holly looked sceptical. 'Not even a mention of it on social.' She put her phone away, as they went into the classroom.

'Maybe it's just too new!' said Azra. 'Which is sort of exciting. Anyway, Cassie's going to ask her neighbour about KW and get more info, aren't you?'

Cassie went red. 'If I get a chance.'

Señor Molina, the Spanish teacher, was writing on the board at the front. The lesson was supposed to be about words to describe your family. But when no one would shut up about the school uniform design, Señor Molina shifted focus and said they could learn the vocab for clothes instead. He wrote on the board:

La blusa: a blouse or shirt

La falda: a skirt

Azul: blue

Cassie looked at Holly. She was throwing her arms

out and saying: '*Me gusta el color!* Because it totally goes with my hair.'

'And the same for the rest of us,' said Cassie. '*Me gusta* a neutral colour like *azul* that suits everyone.'

She'd meant to say it just to Azra, Jules and a couple of the others who were on the same table. But it had come out louder than she intended.

Jules clapped. 'Agreed! And if anyone's interested—'

'We're not!' snapped Holly. She looked at Jules. 'We already know that Bevan the cat has got an electric-blue collar and that she looks sensational in it.'

Jules scribbled the vocab into her book.

As Señor Molina wrote up more words to do with clothing, Azra tried to get Holly and Bea back on side.

'I've done a search for uniforms around the world. Actually, there's a super-cute skirt worn at a school in Spain. And guess what? Some pink bubble sleeves are part of a uniform I found in Thailand . . .'

'We can't just take other people's uniform and use it ourselves,' said Bea. She sat up straight.

Holly nodded, authoritatively. 'That's culturally insensitive.'

'It was only a suggestion!' said Azra. She went red.

Señor Molina flicked the screen. He gave a quick rundown of what people wore to school in Spain, and how it was much more causal, with most schools not having a strict uniform at all.

'A splash of bright colour with the navy would be good,' said Jules, when they were supposed to be pointing at their jumpers and saying *el jersey*.

'I love super brights! What are you thinking?' Cassie grabbed one of her felt tips. She drew a little picture of the uniform and began to colour bits in.

'Ooh, yeah! Neon socks,' said Jules.

'Or nineties' jewel tones,' said Cassie. She shaded the tie in emerald and added ruby red dots on the skirt.

Jules was nodding. 'They look like hundreds and thousands.'

Holly leant over. 'No, no, no. The new uniform should be cool and sophisticated. Like the KW headband!

I know you like cosplay, Cassie, but the rest of us don't want to dress like the pick 'n' mix counter!'

Jules rolled her eyes. 'I was thinking maybe a pink tie?'

'Urgh.' Bea's nose screwed up. 'Pink can be really pathetic.'

'We need to resist pinkification,' said Holly, authoritatively. She held her chin up high. 'This is a girls' school; we'd look a total joke if we went pink.'

'No one takes pink seriously,' said Bea.

Well, they did in the 1700s, thought Cassie. *Back then rich men wore pink to show off their power and wealth.*

Fern swung her rainbow bag further up her arm. 'Anyone should be able to wear any colour they like.'

'And what I like is blue,' said Holly firmly.

'Same,' said Cassie, truthfully. 'Maybe in lots of shades? I'm thinking cobalt, bluebell, teal . . .'

Holly laughed. 'Urgh! That sounds like a Frankenstein's monster of a uniform.'

'Maybe with a splash of yellow!' said Jules cheerfully.

'Yellow? For school uniform?' Holly pulled a face. 'I mean, I know some of us think the Winnie-the-Pooh aesthetic is the way to go—'

Bea burst out laughing.

'But yellow is a bad colour for a school uniform, Jules. I don't reckon even your cat would wear it,' said Holly.

'Ha! Honestly, she would wear anything!'

'She'd probably like yellow because it keeps the mice and rats away,' said Cassie, with a smile. 'When you think about it, it's probably a really great colour for cats.'

'Really?' said Jules.

Azra flashed her eyes at Cassie warningly.

'Yes! And for the uniform too, when you think about it. There's this fashion history creator who did a video about a school in Tudor times where pupils wore yellow socks because the colour was meant to stop rats from nibbling their toes at night.'

'Do you make this stuff up?' said Holly, pulling a face.

The bell rang.

Azra tried to catch Holly and Bea on their way to

the canteen. 'Having cool socks would be a good idea though?' she said, looking desperate. 'I think that's what Cassie meant. Hahaha! Don't worry about it though, our uniform design will be really cool.'

Holly held her hand up. 'We're not having a go. We know *you're* into fashion, Azra.'

'Yes, it's good you're on the team,' said Bea. 'And I get why you are with Fern, obviously.'

Bea looked at Fern and did a little bounce.

Fern had pinned her hair up into space buns and covered them with colourful hairnets. It was a typical Fern take on a major trend: she'd just used the netting off a bag of oranges. But Holly and Bea had been raving about how high-end it looked.

'What with your hair and all,' emphasized Bea.

Holly clasped her hands together. 'Which we love.'

Fern ignored them. She was halfway out of the door.

'But as for Cassie Coltsfoot,' Holly said, super loudly. 'She literally knows NOTHING about fashion.'

*

At lunch, Azra was pacing the side of the field. 'We've got to sort this, Cassie. You've got to stop this fixation with the history of fashion and focus on *real* fashion, which means being on-trend. And not just wearing whatever you want.'

'OK,' said Cassie, as she tapped the side of her head. 'Just making a mental note not to wear that Elizabethan ruff tomorrow.'

'It's not a joke.' Azra rubbed her forehead. 'I'm trying so hard to help! Do you want people like Holly and Bea to laugh at you?'

'Of course not, but . . .'

Cassie was sure entire essays could be written about why girls like Holly and Bea laughed at what other girls wear. But she wasn't sure even that was enough to stop her thinking about fashion history.

'I thought they were interested when we talked about KW,' Azra tried to smile. 'Maybe you should concentrate on finding out more about the brand and just forget history for a bit.'

Cassie nodded.

Azra swiped her screen. 'Fashion is about being in the right jeans, in the right place, at the right time. To know what's in, you just have to know where to look.' She held her screen out to Cassie and clicked on a video about the *Eight Pairs of Jeans that you NEED Right Now.*

The thing is, thought Cassie, *it's not just that I'm obsessed with fashion history. Now I'm a Secret KnitWit, everything looks different. Forget jeans! How about the The Skirt of Your Fairytale Dreams?*

Her heart leapt, as she imagined waking up every morning and putting on outfits made by Mrs Khalid and Milo and the others. Clothes that swished and comforted and made you feel amazing. 'And that Is why we have to enter the competition somehow!' she said, out loud.

'We are entering it!' Azra looked frustrated. 'But they're not going to let us have jeans for school uniform.'

Cassie's cheeks went red. 'Sorry! Yes, I just meant . . .'

Azra snapped her phone off. 'OK, change of plan.

How about you find an influencer to copy? No history allowed! They have to be actually alive . . .'

Azra's neck craned the corner, to where people were coming out of the canteen. She explained that copying someone else's look could be helpful when you're working out your own style. 'It could even be someone at school.'

Mira was walking past with her friend Bella. Mira's handknitted scarf was tossed over her shoulder. She had a glittery snake clip in her hair and stompy boots on. Everything about Mira just screamed style. As the light shone through the trees, Mira kicked some fallen leaves, and said something to Bella, which made her laugh, and Cassie felt like she was watching a film.

'Someone like Mira Lal,' breathed Azra. 'Look at what she's wearing. She gets it so right, every time.'

Azra was talking quite loudly, and Mira must have heard her because she suddenly looked over and frowned.

Cassie grinned. She didn't dare wave. Was she meant

to acknowledge Mira at school? Mira hadn't said. But it seemed unfriendly not to. So, Cassie quickly crossed her forefingers over each other, and did a little action, like they were knitting needles.

A second later, when Bella was distracted – she was pointing to something on the field – Mira did pretend knitting back. Azra didn't seem to see it.

Cassie's insides leapt. She felt a rush of KnitWit confidence. 'OK, my style icon is officially Mira Lal. Maybe she'll show us how to knit a cardigan as gorgeous as hers to help us be the uniform fashion designers?'

'Yeah, right!' Azra giggled. 'As if she'd ever talk to us!'

Chapter 5

'Bit of a weird place to meet,' said Azra after school on Tuesday. Fern had asked them to meet her round the back entrance of the canteen. But then she had run out of English Lit – their last lesson of the day – saying there was something she had to do first.

Crowds of students were making their way to the bus stops or were cycling or walking home. Cassie and Azra looked around them. They weren't even sure they were allowed to hang out near the canteen.

Azra looked worried. 'If we get told off, it's Fern's fault.'

'Here she is!' said Cassie, with relief.

Fern was backing out of the doorway. She was struggling to carry a massive box – stacked with bread rolls, pizza, waffles and brownies. 'Thanks everyone. See you tomorrow!'

She threw the box down on the floor. 'That's pretty heavy.' Fern pulled a couple of tote bags out of her satchel. She bobbed down on the floor and began to unload the food into the bags. 'Sorry, won't be a sec.'

Azra's eyes were wide. 'What are you doing?'

Fern shoved the last few waffles in. 'I collect the leftovers at the end of the day and take them to a cafe in town.'

Azra pulled a face. 'That's a bit off,' she mouthed to Cassie. She looked at Fern. 'How much money do you make?'

'Nothing!' Fern laughed. 'I'm taking them to the zero-waste cafe! They give away any leftover food from schools or supermarkets or wherever.'

'So, it's free?' said Azra. Her eyes slid to the bag of waffles. She looked hesitant. 'It's just that I didn't bring a snack and I'm usually home by now—'

'Help me carry it and you can have one.' Fern screwed her nose up in concentration. 'I think it would be OK for me to give you one because technically you'd be a volunteer . . .'

'I'm sure it is.' Azra quickly grabbed a bag.

The three of them sat down on a bench under the biggest oak tree. The acorns weren't ripe yet but some of the leaves were already edged with gold. There was a squirrel bouncing along the branches, pigeons pecking at the grass beside the trunk, and a notice at the bottom, right beside a badger hole, saying it had been planted in 1897 to mark the Diamond Jubilee of Queen Victoria.

At this time of day, the school was super quiet. There was a game of football at the far end of the field, and there was a Nature Club going along the hedgerows looking for early elderberries and signs of hedgehogs. Mostly, though, the afternoon felt rather empty and calm.

'Thanks for that,' said Azra finally, finishing her waffle and dusting icing sugar off her hands.

'You're welcome.' Fern rolled an acorn between her palms, like it was a massage stone. 'I've been thinking about how we can use the project to raise awareness of fashion crimes.'

'Fashion crimes?' Azra's eyes brightened. 'Like wearing ankle socks over tights or not styling your tie properly?' She touched her own tie, which was neat, wide and tucked into her jumper. According to Azra, this aesthetic was called Top Set Energy because it was inspired by her Maths teacher, who wore scarves under vee-necks. Cassie wore her tie in the traditional long way, which Azra said was totally fine because Cassie was in the bottom set.

'I'm here for that!' said Azra. 'Our design needs to put a new spin on the age-old uniform. We need an outfit that's sophisticated, iconic, in fashion—'

Fern laughed. 'I don't care about fashion! I hate trends. Can't stand labels . . .'

Azra pulled her notebook onto her lap.

'I hate it when people make others feel bad about what they wear,' said Fern, with feeling. 'When I say fashion crimes I mean—'

Cassie jumped in. 'Like rolling your skirt up? I don't think that's a crime, obviously, but I know girls get into trouble for it. Emily says nearly everyone has a detention by summer term because they've naturally grown taller and their skirt suddenly looks short.'

'Sort of,' said Fern. 'The school rules are sexist, and the skirt length is part of that. But the real fashion crime is how the school uniform is wrecking the planet. I'm talking about how it needs to be better for the climate.' Fern was counting on her fingers. 'For animals, and for people . . .'

Azra took a deep breath. 'Well, obviously everyone loves animals and the climate, and I'm interested in *people*, too, and so I've asked *people* what fashion trends they're into.'

She ceremoniously opened her notebook. After a moment or two Azra filled Fern and Cassie in on everything she'd heard that morning, apart from how everyone loved the way Fern had put ribbons in her trainers instead of laces.

'So, we're talking frills, no skirt-length rules and fairy core?' said Fern.

Azra picked up an acorn from the grass. She tried to pull the cup bit off the bottom but it was too green and fresh.

'Which is all great, by the way!' Fern pulled a pile of papers out of her satchel. She lifted her jumper. 'I've been looking into the school rules actually, which are a crime in themselves.'

Azra swallowed hard.

'There are so many more rules for girls!' Fern began to list them. 'We're not allowed clingy shirts or short skirts, which show off our bodies . . .'

Fern waved the papers. She explained how she had requested the official uniform guidelines not just from school but from Pipson Boys School too, so she could compare. 'Says here a short skirt can lead to others being able to see things they don't want to.'

Cassie felt a surge of emotion. 'There's a whole section in my fashion history book about schoolgirls' clothing! Ever since girls were allowed to go to school, the uniform was plain and restricted because people didn't want to encourage us to have pride in what we wear or get unwanted attention—'

'It's so wrong.' Fern jumped up from the bench again and wiggled around doing a comedy dance. 'How is my body offensive in a skirt? Why should my body be restricted? Who's seeing something they don't want to?'

'OMG! Sit down!' Azra looked around her furiously. 'This is totally irrelevant. We're supposed to be designing a new uniform not campaigning against the old one.'

'It *is* relevant! That's the point,' said Fern. 'We're still dealing with those stupid sexist ideas now. There's nothing in here,' she waved at the boys' guidelines, 'saying they can't wear tight shirts or that they must wear vests and boxer shorts or whatever.'

Cassie laughed. 'Urghh!'

Azra covered her face with her hands.

Fern's eyes were scanning the papers. 'Do you know what? There should only be one uniform rule, and that's to wear something you love that's climate friendly. OK, technically that's two rules.' She pointed at Cassie's jumper. But instead, we're told to wear jumpers made of microfibres that slip into the sea . . .'

'What?' Azra looked confused.

Fern launched into a rant about how the tiny plastic particles in their clothes leaked into the water when they were washed – as well as into the air – and that water ends up in the sea, and the tiny particles of fibre get eaten by fish and birds.

'That's a true fashion crime,' said Fern. 'The sweaters we wear to school are made of the exact stuff that ends up being eaten by fish.'

'Right . . .' said Azra.

'That does sound bad,' said Cassie.

Fern sucked her cheeks in to look like the mouth of a fish and wiggled her lips in and out. She leant down and pretended to eat the sleeve of Cassie's jumper.

Cassie giggled. Fern had a mesmerizing, almost clown-like quality to the way she moved and walked. It was hard not to look at her or want to join in with the excitement.

Cassie raised her eyebrows to Azra. 'Makes sense, though! I mean, we shouldn't be wearing fish food sweaters . . .'

'No,' said Azra, sounding super annoyed. 'We should be designing a uniform.' She looked at Cassie's headband. 'I thought you were going to be better at this! What with KW and everything?'

Cassie pulled a face. 'I told you it's a new brand . . . it's not like I know the . . . design team that well.'

Fern leapt up. 'We don't really need a design! We just need a fabric to make jumpers with that doesn't hurt fish! And to help people see why that's the design that should win, we can start a campaign: *Say No to Fish Food Sweaters!*'

'No,' said Azra loudly.

'Exactly!' said Fern.

Azra made a face. 'I meant no to the campaign.'

'We can make it so fun,' said Fern. 'OK! How about we

make some stickers and put them on people's jumpers?'

'How about we don't!' said Azra. 'That's a real crime. What if we damaged someone's jumper?'

'I'll make the stickers at home. They will be totally recyclable. I'll just use a flour and water paste or I'll write things over old blank stickers or something . . .' She grinned. 'Fish Food! That's what we can write on them. I'll do the stickering if you don't want to.' She clapped her hands. 'This is going to be amazing.'

'No it's not! That's like the total opposite of a winning idea!' Azra looked ready to explode. She hugged her notebook to her chest. 'Because I'm telling you that Fish Food stickers is not what the *people* want, and I am the one who has asked the—'

'It's not the only thing we can do,' Cassie said, quickly. 'I'm sure that's just one part of it. We can work on a new design, Az, and meanwhile Fern can—'

'Save the world! Or the fish anyway.' Fern picked up the bags of baked goods.

Cassie forced a smile. 'Great!' She looked at Azra.

'I'm sure we'll come up with a cool design and also,' she nodded encouragingly at Fern, 'like you say, make this a real win for the fish . . .'

Fern did the funny fish face again. She pretended to swim off, the bags slung over her arms. 'Fank you!' she shouted with her wobbly mouth.

A day or two later, Cassie and Emily arrived home from school. They were throwing their bags down in the hallway when they heard their parents' voices.

Emily hesitated. 'Wait.'

Cassie groaned. Mum and Dad were back from leading an Adrenalyn Roman wall-climbing day. Even from the hallway Cassie and Emily could feel the energy bouncing off the walls.

Mum and Dad were doing a post-match analysis of how the day had gone. Cassie peered into the hallway, where you could see into the flat. Mum was standing on the sofa pretending to be clinging on to a sandstone wall.

'It was a strong start!' said Dad. 'Loved your whole Friends, Romans, Country Climbers, speech.'

Mum laughed, appreciatively. 'And your idea for lunch on the ledge of the world was genius. Reckon we can roll this one out as a regular?'

Cassie wasn't in the mood. The last couple of days had been exhausting. Azra was hyping on about the uniform redesign like it was going to be launched at the Northern Fashion Week. And Fern had already put a Fish Food sticker on the folder on Mr Jackson's desk. He'd peeled it off and thrown it in the bin without saying anything.

Then Fern had put some over the mirrors in the loos near their form room. Azra had spent a whole break in there, rubbing them off. Fern had been upset but said she supposed 'the cleaners were only doing their job' (she didn't know Azra had been doing it for them). And she'd decided to be more direct: Fern had been handing stickers out in the canteen today and explaining how the students needed to wear jumpers that weren't fish food. At one point, Fern had got quite a crowd of people around her, and Azra had leapt in, with her notebook, to ask whether people liked pleated skirts.

Cassie hoped Fern's campaign had gone well enough that it could finish ASAP. Holly and Bea had pushed past them in the canteen earlier, saying: 'We've heard enough about fish food, we're here to get proper food!' and Azra had gone into a spin about how Fern needed to stay popular. It had taken Cassie the rest of lunch to calm her down.

Now, all Cassie wanted to do was race through her homework so she could flop on her bed and read her fashion history book.

'I wonder if the girls would like to come on the next Roman climbing day—' Mum was saying.

'Maybe,' said Dad. 'You know what, that's given me an idea. Maybe it would be worth asking if their History teacher wanted to book a day with us. Cassie's class are doing a topic on Romans, aren't they?'

'Schools, Adrian! Could be a lucrative new line of business. And we could do with the extra money,' said Mum. 'We could ask the girls. They'll be here any minute.'

'Back up, back up!' hissed Cassie.

Emily clicked the door shut, with them on the outside. She dumped her bag down on the landing. 'Let's do some climbing practice. Want to slide down the pole?'

'Guess it's the fastest way out of here!'

'And the quickest way to feel better,' said Emily. She whipped her school skirt off – underneath she had high-waisted shorts, which made it easier to zip down the pole. Seconds later, she was already at the bottom.

Cassie gripped onto the pole. The steel was cold but smooth – worn down by years of hands holding on to it. As soon as they were old enough to use the fire pole, she and Emily said they'd never use the stairs again. And Emily hadn't. She even slid down the pole in winter, wearing wellies and her big coat.

Cassie did the little jump her sister had taught her to do, then loosened her grip so she could slide down.

A second later her feet hit the bottom, and she nearly went flying into one of the plant pots. She ran back to the top and did it again. This time she bent her knees properly at the end so that she fell with a whoosh. She knew the fire pole was originally there for serious reasons. But having it here at home was so much fun. 'I can't believe I don't always do this!'

'I know! Why do you ever take the stairs? You're the one that's supposed to be into history.' Emily put on a mock serious voice. 'You should observe the traditions of this building.'

'I promise I will.' Cassie felt happier and more relaxed than she had in days. She smiled. Emily was familiar, comforting and the person she most loved hanging out with. *Em is like the clothes equivalent of a favourite pair of pyjamas.*

Cassie sat down on the stairs and pulled out her knitting. 'However, I will now observe another ancient tradition . . .'

She'd started her first solo project – the strap for

Emily's climbing bag. She'd got a pattern online and watched a ton of tutorials (sessions with the KnitWits didn't come around frequently enough for Cassie's liking). It was an historical stitch, more like crochet than knitting, that was used in the early nineteenth century for stitching the costumes of trapeze artists. Cassie knew Emily wasn't going to haul herself up by the bag straps like it was a rock-climbing harness – the bag was only there to carry chalk for dusting hands during the climb – but the super-strength stitch just felt right. It was simple loops but once Cassie learnt the basic stitch, she just had to repeat it over and over.

She'd planned to take her wool out at break. But break had whizzed by with Azra asking people for their views on wide-leg trousers (her latest idea for the uniform fashion design) and Cassie hadn't had the chance.

It was probably a good thing, Cassie told herself. What if someone realized her headband was handmade? What if Mira walked past . . .

She slid her crochet needle into the piece. 'Em, did you know that in the Elizabethan times there were Knitting Schools?'

'No, but I'm glad they've gone.'

'There was this one in Yorkshire, I was reading about it last night. It was going in the eighteenth century, and the girls there knitted 339 stockings in one year. So much nicer than doing stuff like RE and Maths and—'

'I'd rather do Maths than make ancient socks.'

'Ancient socks? Thanks for asking! The oldest surviving knitted socks that I've read about so far are from Egypt and are about nine hundred years old.'

'And we thought Dad's socks were old,' said Emily. 'I'm tuning out now. Got to concentrate on my moves.'

Emily leapt up and climbed halfway up the fire pole and reached over to one of the industrial steel bars that ran across the ceiling. She gripped onto the narrow ridge at the bottom of it, and inched her hands along, swinging her body to get momentum going. A minute later and she was at the main front door of the fire station flats. Emily was focusing so hard on every hand grip on the pipe that she didn't see the door open.

'Careful!' shouted Cassie.

Emily dodged the door just in time. She narrowly avoided slamming right into Mrs Khalid and instead landed on her feet. 'Arghhhhhhh! Sorry!'

'Nearly killed me there!' said Mrs Khalid. She dusted herself down. 'Better luck next time.' She laughed nervously, pretending she hadn't just had a real shock. 'Are you OK?'

'I'm fine!' Emily stood up straight. 'But I'm so sorry for landing on you like that. I think I hurt your toe? Did I hurt your toe?'

'It's still in one piece!' Mrs Khalid smoothed down her coat, which was every colour of autumn. She did a little twist of her ankles. 'You're OK, that's the main thing.'

'Only just.' Emily looked a bit shaken.

Mrs Khalid looked up at the stairs. Cassie had thrown her knitting down and had her hand on her chest. 'I was about to call the emergency services . . .'

Mrs Khalid smiled. 'Talking of that, Cassie, Allan has called an emergency meeting about the competition.'

'The competition? I thought that was off?'

'So did we! But it seems like Allan applied by midnight on Saturday anyway and has put the KnitWits down to produce a garment. We should be cross with him.' Mrs Khalid rolled her eyes. 'But the truth is, most of us love a project like this . . .'

Cassie was on her feet.

'They're upstairs in my flat as we speak.' Mrs Khalid lifted up a shopping bag. 'I had to pop out for more milk. Samira said she'd come later, after Physics Club. She's one of the less-impressed KnitWits,' Mrs Khalid smiled. 'But it's good to have opinions! Why don't you come up for a bit?'

Chapter 6

The second Cassie went into Mrs Khalid's sitting room she was back in the grip of KnitWit mania. Her heart raced. Snuggly yarns, reams of ribbons, zips, threads and glittery fabric were thrown across the velvety green sofa.

On the table, there was a sewing machine already whirling. Serena was doing the hem on her velvet bodice. Apparently, she took her projects with her everywhere, and sewed all through her lunch breaks. Milo's skirt was there too – he'd brought it to show the others how he'd done ruffles on the waistline.

Allan was pacing near the kitchen and doing super-size hand knitting. He wound the yarn up and over his hands and elbows like he was doing a dance. Leta and

Milo were sitting on the floor, flicking through all the KnitWit scrapbooks for inspiration.

There was a sort of buzzy, edgy energy. Everyone was focused, but in a weird, uptight way. Like the atmosphere in class when a teacher announces that there's a test in five minutes.

'Got that oat milk you like, Allan,' said Mrs Khalid.

'You're very kind,' bellowed Allan. He pulled the wool through a loop and dramatically slung the ball over his shoulder.

Mrs Khalid dumped the bag on the table. She smoothed back her hair and flicked the kettle on. 'And Jammie Dodgers for all ...'

'Thanks! We'll need them.' Leta was pointing at a photo of a shawl in the scrapbook. 'We could do this one again? I've still got lots of leftover wool.'

'I remember that one!' Serena shouted over from the table. 'You made it for one of your aunts?'

Leta smiled. 'She still loves it. Or says she does ...'

Cassie sat down beside them. 'It's beautiful!' she

traced her fingers along the photo. It was edged with a delicate knitted lace border. 'That's so pretty.'

'And like you said, you've got the wool,' said Serena. 'That's a start. We'd need to make it longer, though, turn it into a dress. Perhaps keep the style of the shawl, and make it a wrap dress?'

'It could work,' Leta nodded. 'I could teach you to do the edging, Cassie.' She dived into her bag and pulled out a stretch of lace. 'I've been doing this while on the bus to work.' She gave it to Cassie. 'It's not the same as the shawl. But you get the idea.'

'Thanks!' Cassie played with the knitted lace. She tied it around her ankle. *One tiny detail, one total transformation.* She twisted her ankle so she could see the lace at different angles.

'The shawl is brilliant, Leta. And definitely competition worthy.' Milo shook his head. 'But from what I remember, it was a complicated pattern and . . .'

Mrs Khalid cut in. 'Which means the judges would be able to see how complicated the stitches are and would be more impressed?'

Cassie nodded. 'It's like the uniform design at school. Ms Ginty says that if you *make* a skirt or something rather than just draw it, you get points for the extra work.'

Mrs Khalid nodded. 'Good point. We need to all put in as much work as we're able.'

'But I can't knit as well as Leta,' said Milo. 'I'd like to be part of this but I can't do those stitches.'

'I'm better at sewing, so knitting a bit of the shawl each wouldn't really show all of our different skills,' said Serena.

Cassie felt a flutter of nerves. She loved the way this conversation was going. It sounded like they were going to enter – and they should! The KnitWits were so talented. But she didn't want Mira thinking she'd helped make it happen.

She looked at the door. Would Mira be annoyed that Cassie was even sitting here? How long did Physics Club go on for?

'Which is why we can't do the shawl.' Allan took his glasses off and rubbed his eyes. 'We need something that's created in different pieces so we can work on it simultaneously.'

'What, then?' said Serena.

There was a long silence.

'And we need to show innovation.' Allan was dunking biscuits into his tea, two at a time. 'Style, technique and that we're forward thinking . . .'

Milo shut the scrapbook. He sighed loudly. 'This is a tough gig. I'm not sure we're going to be able to do it.'

Mrs Khalid picked up her shrug from the back of the sofa. 'Is there anything we could re-use?'

Cassie's eyes leapt at the sight of the shrug. Mrs Khalid smiled and popped it on Cassie's shoulders.

Cassie stroked it. It was so delicate and flawless it could have been knitted by woodland fairies. No matter what they were up to – embroidering velvet bodies, knitting chunky robes – the KnitWits had a knack for making clothes that just made you feel better.

Serena nodded approvingly. 'Looks like it was made for you!'

A dress made for me, thought Cassie.

'Back to the task in hand.' Allan tipped his head. 'We could re-use something but only if we create it into something new. We need to upload photos of the progress as part of the final submission.'

Milo shrugged. 'We haven't really got anything anyway.'

'OK.' Serena switched off the sewing machine. She pushed her hair out of her eyes. 'Here's something we do at work when we're starting a project and want to stay positive.'

Cassie didn't know exactly what Serena did for a job but it was something at a creative agency. She definitely had the right aesthetic for that. She was wearing a chunky half-zip jumper, with a boxy silhouette and dark jeans.

Serena passed around pieces of paper and asked everyone to write down one reason for wanting to enter and one thing they could bring to the project.

'This is just an exercise to help us all focus!' she said. She sat knees crossed on the floor. 'So write down what you really want to do. Be honest.'

Leta pretended she was thinking aloud as she wrote. 'Allan's an idiot to get us into this mess . . .'

Serena laughed. 'Not that honest! But, if you could think of one thing you can do for the competition, then write it down.'

God, this is so cool, thought Cassie.

Cassie crossed hers out about three times, so in the end her paper was difficult to read.

Happy to do anything to help!

Can make tea!

I could do some sewing as well but you'd have to teach me how

I could donate my button box in case there's anything you want to use from it

I could write little signs about the historical stitches

~~Enter the competition because you're~~
~~AMAZING, talented and friendly and you're~~
~~going to WIN! (is that too many reasons??)~~

She paused. She knew Mira didn't want the KnitWits to be in the competition. But everything had changed. Their names were down; they'd entered. That wasn't Cassie's fault. And she really, really wanted to be a part of it.

She felt the comforting softness of the shrug around her shoulders, and the delicate lace around her ankle. *These clothes*, thought Cassie, *they make me feel as good as my fringed twenties' dress. If the KnitWits win the competition* . . .

She knew the main problem Mira had with the competition was the idea of people at school finding out about the KnitWits. But there must be a way to enter without anything going out on social media. How could she tell the KnitWits how badly she wanted to be the model? How could she *not*?

'OK! All done?' Cassie held the paper on her knee where no one could see it. Quickly, she fired off what she could offer:

I truly love the clothes you make and I love fashion and history (and especially fashion history) more than anything (apart from my family, friends, and my 1920s'-style dress). And if you're looking for a model, I'd love it to be me.

A minute later, Serena collected them up.

'Thanks,' said Allan. He held his hands out. 'Just want to say I'm sorry, folks. For stressing you out and putting down our names for the competition before it was agreed.'

Everyone sort of shrugged or shook their heads.

'It's OK,' said Leta. 'We know that winning the competition would mean a lot to you.'

Milo nodded. 'Winning an award would help you leave your job, and make a go of sewing professionally?'

'Well, it wouldn't hurt,' Allan coughed. 'But I can't do it without you all.'

'And we love a challenge,' said Mrs Khalid. 'But as everyone's just said, the timing is tight.'

'Thanks for trying anyway.' Allan took a deep breath. 'I think I'll write to the judges. Withdraw the application—'

'No!' The word was out of Cassie's mouth before she knew it. 'There's got to be a way to enter!' Her heart pounded. 'You can do this! I know you can.'

Leta touched her headscarf. She looked uncertain. 'I don't think we can.'

'What if . . .' Cassie's brain was racing. She suddenly jumped up. 'Maybe you don't have to feel the pressure to do anything new. You've got the fabric; you've started all the different pieces. It just needs to be stitched up!'

She pointed to Milo's skirt, which was draped over the back of the sofa. 'Can I borrow this? And these?' She gathered up Serena's bodice, sleeves that Leta had made, Mrs Khalid's shrug, and other bits and pieces made by Suze and Kass, semi-regular KnitWits attendees, who had slung them on the table.

She slipped the bodice on over her top and stepped into the skirt. She carefully slipped her hand into the sleeves and on the other side of her she draped Mrs Khalid's shrug. There was a scarf on the table. Cassie tied it around her waist to bring the bodice and skirt together and kept her headband on. The colours were mesmerizing. Shimmering shades of blue that merged together, like a dusky blue sky fading into the sea.

A minute later, Cassie was standing in front of the KnitWits, with her arms outstretched. Her eyes were bright. 'This could work!'

There was a sharp intake of breath.

Serena looked amazed. 'That is what I call a vision.'

'The key to the look is not hiding that it's been made by different people, with different fabrics and talents,' said Cassie. She was talking fast, everything coming out in a rush. 'We can just stitch it all together.'

Milo clapped. 'I can see it!'

Leta grabbed a ball of wool. Serena and Milo were nodding and chattering about adjustments and how long it might take. Mrs Khalid passed Cassie a biscuit.

'Only thing is,' Allan was stroking his chin, 'all the blues are different.'

Cassie looked excited. 'That's OK! Back in Victorian times, different shades of blue were used on the same evening dresses. The lighter blues and the golds,' she pointed to the bodice, 'like this one, were added to make the fabric shine in the gaslight. It's like the communal cardi you made for Mira!' She threw her arms out. 'You've already got everything you need, everyone just needs to do their bit—'

The atmosphere in the room was charged with excitement and relief, and hope. Cassie felt like that moment when you're untangling a necklace and you suddenly see where the knot is and know how to undo it.

'Let's go for it,' said Serena.

There was a chorus of agreement. Everyone was

talking about how quickly they could get their part done.

'We'll need shoes too,' said Leta. 'Does anyone have a pair that would go with the dress?'

Mrs Khalid nodded. 'Depends on who's modelling it, but there's always my old shoe collection'.

Leta did a little clap. 'Perfect!'

Mrs Khalid had a vintage shoe collection? Cassie gasped.

'I travelled a lot when I was younger,' explained Mrs Khalid, as she talked about the shoes.

Cassie's heart raced. Every pair sounded incredible. Boots bought one cold winter in Berlin! Sparkly heels that had danced at parties in Lahore! Slingback mules worn to a conference in Croatia! Sandals that had trekked through the Atlas Mountains!

Mrs Khalid and Leta began to throw in their suggestions for footwear that would suit the dress.

Cassie tried to look at Mrs Khalid's feet without looking like she was looking at Mrs Khalid's feet. She was wearing thick socks and clogs. It was impossible to tell what shoe size she was.

'Got it!' said Leta suddenly. 'The silver trainers. They're rare, vintage and still in immaculate condition.'

'I'll bring them to the meeting on Saturday,' said Mrs Khalid. Her hands were clasped together and her eyes bright.

Cassie's excitement ratcheted up a level.

She swung the midnight skirt up in the air. *Wow! Imagine looking down and seeing vintage silver trainers on my feet.* The sheen fabric would pick up the starry sparkles on the skirt, and metallic trainers were the perfect mix of understated, effortless glamour.

A minute later, and Leta and Milo began packing their knitting away. Serena unplugged the sewing machine. Mrs Khalid gathered the mugs.

'The blue dress is, as we say, officially on the needle,' Allan said, sounding relieved.

Cassie was still holding everything up in front of her. A velvet bodice, a swish of the skirt. She said to herself,

The Girl in the Blue Dress with the Silver Trainers.

'All we need to do now,' said Allan, 'is find someone willing to be our model—'

Just at that moment, the door opened. It was Mira. She dumped her bag on the floor. 'Okaaay.' Mira's eyes narrowed as she took in the scene. 'What did I miss?'

Chapter 7

'I'll see Cassie out!' said Mira, a few minutes later, once the others had filled her in about the exciting last-minute entry to the competition.

'No need! I'm only going downstairs.' Cassie threw off the skirt and gathered her things as fast as she could.

'I insist.' Mira marched down the landing.

Cassie moved so fast she tripped over the rug and spilt a tiny bit of tea in her cup. She had to go back to the kitchen and grab a cloth. It was only a drop, but it threw her into a panic. Mrs Khalid's flat was immaculate. How could she have been so clumsy? She ineffectually rubbed away at the carpet, until Milo came over with a bowl of water and vinegar, and told her to let him sort it.

Outside the Coltsfoot front door, Mira was waiting for

her. Arms folded, eyeliner like dark rings thrown around eyes so angry they were on fire. Cassie nearly did what Emily did when Cassie was fit to explode. Emily would pick up the ancient fire hose still attached to the wall and pretend to put out the flames of her temper.

But this was no time for jokes. Mira was furious.

'Why did you do it? I've told you we can't have them entering this competition!'

'It's not as if I called the meeting! They were all there when I got home, Mira, honestly. They were going to enter the competition whether I was there or not.' She thought for a moment. 'In fact, they already had! Allan entered without anyone else knowing.'

'But not with *the blue dress*,' Mira emphasized the words like they were something bad.

Cassie's face crumpled. 'What's wrong with the blue—'

'You know what's wrong with it!'

Cassie stared at her.

'It's absolutely outstanding, Cassie! That's the

problem. It's obvious that the blue dress is exactly the sort of thing that could win.'

'So what's the . . .'

'Why couldn't you just have let them knit a poncho or a shawl? Something that shows talent, but isn't a winner?' Mira's hands were thrown out wildly as she made her points. Her eyeliner was smudging in the corner. 'Wait—'

Cassie almost thought Mira was having second thoughts and had come up with an idea to somehow make everything OK.

'Who's modelling it?'

Cassie paused. 'I don't know.'

'You don't know who might be modelling a dress that you've basically designed and were holding up in front of yourself?'

'I didn't say anything about *me* being the model!' said Cassie truthfully. 'I just gave them the idea for the dress.'

Mira stared hard. 'You sure?'

'Of course I'm sure!' Cassie's cheeks went bright red. 'It was only a way of showing everyone how the outfit could work . . .' She could hear how guilty her voice sounded.

Mira's face softened.

Cassie gulped. 'I won't even come to the KnitWits on Saturday if you don't want me there.'

'Excuse me?' Mrs Khalid had come down the stairs and was standing across the landing. She glared at Mira.

Mira's face flushed. 'I didn't say that Cassie shouldn't come. I promise! I didn't, did I, Cassie?'

'She didn't, Mrs Khalid.'

'Good. Because you should be there on Saturday, Cassie. In fact, we expect it!'

Mira looked upset. 'All I meant was to remind her that—'

'Maybe you need reminding that the competition is a CommunKnitty project. And the KnitWits is an inclusive, supportive group. And if you can't respect that, Samira, maybe it's you who shouldn't come on Saturday.'

A minute later, Cassie hurled herself through the front door. It wasn't until she had gone into her own bedroom, thrown herself face down on her pillow, that she realized the piece of paper with her ideas about what she could contribute for the competition was still on the table.

Chapter 8

'Don't keep twisting round like that. We're way past the time you can get off the bus and run home for your PE kit.'

Cassie threw herself down on the bus seat. 'Stop shouting at me!'

'Calm down,' said Emily in a low hiss. 'And *you* stop shouting.' As the bus veered around the duck pond – about ten minutes away from Pipson High – Emily split a tea cake and passed half to Cassie. She looked annoyed. 'I don't even get how you didn't realize you have PE today?'

Cassie jumped up in her bus seat. 'Probably because I had the worst night's sleep ever because I've ruined Mira Lal's life.'

Emily put her hands to her forehead. 'Can you *not*?'

'Why are you being like this? You were so nice to me last night!'

Emily had heard Cassie sobbing and spent ages in her room, until she felt better.

'Because I don't like bus emergencies. And I don't think it's Mira Lal's fault that you didn't check your timetable.'

'My timetable . . .' Cassie stuffed the tea cake in her mouth to hold it. She scrambled in her bag. She pulled out her phone and looked up which lessons she had that day. 'OMG! Art and Geography! I've not done my Art homework—'

'You haven't done your *Art* homework?' Emily looked super annoyed.

Art was Emily's favourite lesson, apart from gym. She'd been telling Cassie for years how much she was going to love the Art rooms at Pipson High. When Cassie said she preferred the History classroom, with its Tudor displays and cardboard Battle of Hastings shields, Emily seemed to take it as a personal affront. 'You can't just not hand in homework; you're going to get a detention!'

'Alright, *Mum*!' said Cassie. She bit her lip. 'It's too late now, anyway.'

Emily shoved the last of the tea cake into her mouth. She dusted her hands. 'It's not too late. We've got a few minutes. Just do a quick sketch of whatever it is—'

'I mean, it's too late because I've also got to do my Geography five facts about the River Dee—'

'You're getting worse.' Emily's eyes widened. 'I think your brain has been undone by all the knitting.'

Cassie nodded. A flood of tears came into her eyes. 'Honestly, Em, that's not a bad description.' Her throat began to tighten. 'But it's more like everything feels tangled up like a ball of wool that's full of knots, and that my feelings are going round and round and getting more and more knotted. And it's like there are different balls of wool all getting messed up together.' She sniffed. 'There's the Azra tangle, and the whole year seven ball of feelings.' She slumped right down on the bus seat. 'And like I said last night, when I think about Mira—'

Emily flicked her hands. 'We haven't got time for this. Is that your sketchbook?' She pointed to the pile of things on the bus seat that had come from Cassie's bag. 'Hand it over.'

Emily took the book and pulled out a pencil. 'Start writing something about the Dee for Geography. And I really shouldn't do this and you'd better not tell Mum and Dad but . . .' she stared at Cassie, 'what are you meant to have drawn?'

'A self-portrait.'

As the bus swung round the corner, Emily's pencil swept across the page. She threw the sketchbook back.

'Oh my god, EMILY!' Cassie flung it down. 'I look completely demented!'

Emily had captured Cassie brilliantly: there was her cute nose, and heart-shaped face and the eyes were so realistic you'd think they could blink. But her hands were stuck on either side of her cheeks – in a shocked pose – and her mouth gaped open.

'Calm down!' said Emily. 'Five deep breaths.'

Cassie began to inhale. Her eyes filled with tears. She let the air out. 'I asked for a self-portrait. This looks like a rip-off of that horrible painting called *The Scream*!'

'No, it doesn't! It wasn't my fault you had your emergency face on.'

'No one has eyebrows that arched, Em! They're practically triangles.' Cassie stared at the picture. Her heart rate shot up. 'And even if I did look that . . . panicked, which I DEFINITELY don't, there is NO WAY, I'd draw myself like that. Which means that when Mrs Dyer asks me to explain it, I'll have no choice but to say that you—'

Emily grabbed the sketchbook back. She toned down the expression and gave the portrait a prettier turn of the lips – which was truer to Cassie anyway – and straightened out her eyebrows.

'Thanks, Emily.'

The bus pulled up outside school. Cassie's stomach turned. 'And you're 100 per cent sure that you don't have your PE kit in your locker? That I definitely can't borrow it?'

'I had PE yesterday. So, I stuck my kit in the wash last night.' They went through the main gates.

Cassie sighed. Emily was so organized it was exhausting. 'What am I going to do?'

'There's only one thing for it. Borrow something from Lost Property.'

When the bell for lunch went, everyone sped to the hall towards a delicious smell wafting down the corridor. A group of year eights were doing a fundraiser, selling bags of flavoured popcorn, and the messaging board said there was lots of plain salted popcorn available but that the salted caramel was Limited Edition.

'LIMITED EDITION!' Holly pushed past everyone as 7B came out of French class. 'Right, we need to move fast.'

'Says here if we're early we can get three bags for the

price of two.' Bea was on her phone.

'So that's me, Bea and . . .' Holly looked around, as if she was about to bestow a great honour on someone.

'Me!' said Azra.

Cassie felt a pang of annoyance. Azra really needed to stop trying to get in with Holly and Bea.

Holly pointed at Azra. 'You're in.' She looked around at everyone else, none of whom had their hand up. 'The decision is final!'

'Ooh, that's me!' Azra was hopping around, looking excited. 'I'll share mine with you, Cassie.'

Cassie smiled. 'It does smell good but—'

'Come on!' Holly beckoned her. 'You're buying one of the two bags, by the way, Azra. I'm having the free one.'

Azra spluttered. 'I thought you meant we'd split the cost?'

'Quick!' said Holly. 'Limited edition is selling fast.'

Azra grabbed Cassie. 'The hall is this way . . .'

'I can't come, Az. I've forgotten my PE kit, so I'm going to borrow something from Lost Property.'

'Lost Property?' Azra shrieked. 'That stuff stinks!'

Cassie flushed. 'So does getting a detention.'

'But what about the popcorn?' Azra looked torn. 'I've gone and promised them now—'

Cassie sighed inwardly. It would serve Holly right to have to buy her own popcorn. And it would be good to have some company at Lost Property. But it wasn't worth making a fuss.

'Just go. I'll meet you later, on the bench.'

Azra headed off in the direction of the salted caramel smell. Most people had wandered off by now to the canteen, library or lunchtime. But Fern was on the floor on her knees. She was looking for her hair clip.

Cassie picked up the clip, which had skittered right to the other side of the corridor.

'Thanks! Hey, by the way, heard you talking about Lost Prop,' said Fern, amiably. Fern had such a cheerful way of walking. All springy and fun. She always looked like she was going in the direction she wanted. 'I'm kind of interested to see what's in there.'

'I'm a bit nervous to see what Mrs Lane is like,' said Cassie, with a grimace. 'My sister Emily says she's a bit scary.'

Fern laughed. 'Let's find out.'

Mrs Lane looked Cassie up and down. She had a pen dangling from her mouth, her eyes were unamused. 'What do you want? First aid? A dinner money loan? If it's spare tights you want, I haven't got any,' she said, like she was the emergency services.

'Hello!' said Cassie brightly. 'Lost Property, please.'

'I've just put it away.' There was a grumble. Mrs Lane lifted up a tablet with a form pre-loaded. She pushed her purply-silver hair out of her eyes. 'But if it's a phone, wallet or keys, I'll need you to fill in your details before I show you what's in there.'

'It's not that I've lost something. It's more that I need to find something . . .'

'This isn't a box of freebies, you know,' said Mrs Lane, sternly. 'These things belong to someone.'

'I just need to borrow—'

'I'm sorry!' said Mrs Lane sarcastically. 'Is this a library?'

'Is that a photo of you?' said Fern. She was on her tiptoes, peering into the office. She pointed to a photo of a school play that looked like it had been taken years ago. Though not as far back as the costumes, which were all feather boas, suits and party frocks. 'The third girl from the left?'

'How can you tell that?' Mrs Lane's expression changed.

Fern shrugged. 'The smile?'

Mrs Lane pulled it down from the wall. She turned it around and started telling them all about the school play of *Bugsy Malone* back in the nineties, when she'd been at Pipson High.

'I love your dress,' said Cassie. 'It's so accurate, the way the neckline is pleated at the edges. That's a real 1920s' trend.'

Mrs Lane looked pleased. 'I made the costume myself

during Textiles. And I did research real dresses. Well, you two are quite the observers . . .'

A couple of minutes later, she put the picture back on the wall. 'Now, why don't you tell me what you need.'

'No, it's OK!' said Cassie, quickly. 'I didn't mean to put you out and I genuinely love the dress in the picture.'

Mrs Lane smiled. 'I could tell. Go on then, what do you need?'

'A PE kit. I've forgotten mine. I just need it for one lesson, then I'll give it back.'

Mrs Lane looked torn. 'I'm not meant to let you lot do this any more. If I keep lending people things, apparently, you'll never develop personal responsibility. On the other hand, you're only in your first term . . .'

Mrs Lane was rummaging through the box.

She shook her head. 'You're out of luck,' she said finally. 'One of the new admin officers went through it the other day. No idea where they've gone and put the spare kits.'

Cassie's chest was tight. Could she say she had a

headache? It wasn't really a lie. She *did* feel sick at the thought of getting a detention.

There was an awkward silence.

Cassie was about to ask if she could have a little lie down in First Aid and maybe even a glass of water when Mrs Lane jangled a key. She lowered her voice. 'Do you know the old stockroom, near the Sports Hall?'

Cassie nodded. There was a door there, permanently locked.

'It's a room really, not a cupboard. It's where Lost Property used to go to die. It's full of old clothes and—'

'Old clothes?' It felt like a flight of butterflies had swarmed in Cassie's chest.

'Confiscated items like leg warmers and fluorescent socks from detentions gone by, apparently. I've not been in there for years. And if there are any PE tops in there, they'll be the old style ... but if you're desperate?'

'I am.'

Cassie's heart started beating faster.

Mrs Lane gave her the key. She suddenly looked

concerned. 'Come and tell me when you're finished, though, please. I shouldn't really let you girls go in there. No one has sorted through that stuff in decades.'

'OK, we've only got a few minutes and I need a PE top,' Cassie said as she put the key into the lock.

'Go!' said Fern. 'I'm on it!'

After a minute of stumbling around finding the light switch, their eyes adjusted.

Cassie nearly fell back against the door. Her jaw dropped open. 'OMG, this is INSANE!'

Stuff was everywhere. Old-fashioned trench coats, puffer jackets and peacoats were packed into a cupboard. Shelves were stacked with books, stationery, pairs of swimming googles and vintage Snoopy flasks, and leg warmers were dangling down, like woolly stalactites.

There were boxes on the floor, heaped with old trainers, shoes and ancient Doc Marten boots, just thrown on top. She squealed. An old bike was propped up against the wall.

Fern wheeled it out and put her feet on the pedals. The stockroom was big enough for her to cycle a few turns of the wheels. 'This is so cool. A retro bike! I wonder whose it was?'

'They can't just have lost it, can they?' Cassie frowned.

'Maybe it was confiscated.'

'No! What did they do that was so bad that an actual bike was confiscated and never given back?'

Fern suddenly leapt up and waved her arms up and down. 'Maybe their ghost is in here and will tell us, woo-hoo!'

'Very funny. . .'

It's actually a bit spooky in here, so please don't do that, thought Cassie.

Fern wheeled it back to the wall and propped it up. 'What have you got?'

'Hair accessories!' Cassie's hands were in a box that was a lucky dip of bobbles, a jade-green butterfly clip, and old ballet-style bands. She pulled out a scrunchie in blue crushed velvet. Cassie's heart raced. If she told

Azra she'd got this in Claire's, she'd believe her. *Actually, it might be from there,* she thought. *Circa early nineties!*

She pulled a piece of hair to turn into a short side pony but the scrunchie kept falling out. She pushed the scrunchie onto her wrist to try it on, before putting it back into the box. What else was in here?

She turned around to see Fern wearing a lemon puffer jacket. 'I mean, I didn't think yellow was my colour.' Fern smoothed down the sleeves. She giggled. 'How wrong I was!'

'Eighties' vibes!' said Cassie.

Everywhere they looked there was something else to try on. Coats, jackets – including a tweed one with a ton of badges on it, with slogans like *Save-the-Whales* – and a pair of tie-dye leggings, a box stuffed with neon socks, tights and stripy witch-style socks; and one random roller skate.

Fern was rummaging through a box on the far side.

'Tell you what's great about these clothes, Cas! They're not synthetic, they're woollen and old so they're spun better, which means they don't end up in the ocean.'

Cassie pulled a leg warmer out of the box. 'That's cool, Fern! By the way, do you think you're done with the Fish Food campaign? I mean, I've heard lots of people talking about it.' *Especially Azra, who won't stop complaining about it.*

'No! Definitely not.'

'Really?'

'The problem is that people are totally into it when I explain what the stickers mean. No one wants jumpers that hurt fish. They're all, "Oh no, this is SOOO bad, and how can we let this terrible pollution happen to our oceans?" And things like that. But then . . . this is the thing I don't get . . . they just carry on wearing the jumpers.'

Cassie suddenly felt really hot and uncomfortable. 'But we can't just dump our jumpers.' She looked at hers. Mum and Dad had only bought it a few weeks ago.

'And sometimes, when I close my eyes,' Fern said, in

a really sad voice, 'I imagine this shoal of fish swimming past, with big, disappointed faces, and they're looking at me and saying . . .' Fern sucked her cheeks in, and wobbled her lips, '"Why doesn't anyone care?"'

Cassie felt a wave of emotion. She pulled her jumper over her head.

OK, concentrate, Cassie told herself. *I can't wear that jumper any more but I still need to find a PE kit.* 'Have you seen anything sporty?'

Fern pointed towards a box on the far side, labelled PE Kit.

Cassie laughed. 'Why didn't you say anything?'

They both dug through the box together.

There were PE tops from what looked like every decade since Pipson High was founded. Each one had a girl's name embroidered along the top instead of written on the label.

'This one looks clean-ish.' Fern held up a top. The shape and fit looked similar to the one they wore, but the fabric was mesh with tiny holes in it. The words:

Kitty McLister were sewn in chain stitch across the top pocket.

'Thanks! And thank you, Kitty McLister!' said Cassie. 'Wherever you are today.'

'Gym skirt?' Fern threw one over. 'It seems Kitty left the whole outfit behind!'

'Gym skirts? Wow!'

It was very short. The label looked vintage – eighties, maybe, or even earlier. It was a wrap style, with a long length of material to wind around your waist, a plain front panel, and pleats back and side.

'Technically they are still uniform. According to the rules you can wear them, as they've never officially been removed from the list of PE kit. It's just that everyone wears sports leggings. But if you're desperate.'

'I'm desperate to wear one. I love them!' Cassie found the button on the inside of the waistband and fastened it so the skirt wrapped around her.

'This will shake up PE chic!' Cassie did a twirl.

Fern laughed. 'Do you know what? I'm going to wear

one too!' She put it on over her leggings.

'I know that retro trend is ending,' said Cassie. She clapped her hands. 'But wearing it over your leggings looks so good . . .'

Fern spun around, her arms flung out wide. Her pleated skirt flipped out. The name Sarah Warner was stitched along the hem at the front. She laughed. 'I love the embroidered names too.'

The bell went.

'Are we done?' said Fern.

Cassie nodded. She went to open the door but her eyes caught sight of a rounded shape on the top shelf nearest the door. Her stomach somersaulted.

'NO. WAY!' It was a beret. Her heart raced. An original Pipson 1960s beret. Exactly the same as the photos in the library. She spun it around in her hand. 'I can't believe I'm holding one! A Pipson Original.'

Fern looked excited. 'It's like a blueberry. Try it on!'

Cassie stuck it on. It fitted her head like it was made for her.

'Do you think I could borrow it?' Cassie turned around in the hat. It felt amazing. 'Would anyone mind? It's just so . . .'

'We could always ask Mrs Lane. But like she said no one has been bothered about this stuff for years.'

'How can they not be bothered?' Cassie did another spin. *Talk about channelling your inner French goddess!* 'I'm going to make this my signature style. For ever! Will you check those old school uniform rules? See if they ever officially dropped the beret?'

'So what if they did? We're allowed to wear things on our heads now, aren't we? I say go for it.'

Cassie smiled. She picked up her bag. She suddenly remembered she hadn't gone to the bench to meet Azra. *OMG!* Cassie checked her phone. Three messages:

> **Azra: I'm at the bench!**

> **Azra: Why aren't you at the bench?**

Azra: I'm leaving the bench. Message me.

Cassie suddenly felt nervous. If Azra hadn't been mad enough about the popcorn situation, she'd be ready to explode at her now. 'Are we really going to PE like this, Fern?'

Fern tugged the flap of her gym skirt. 'Actually, I think you'll find I'm called Sarah Warner.'

Cassie laughed. 'Good to know.'

Fern held the door open. 'After you, Kitty McLister.'

As they set off towards the Admin office Cassie fell into step with Fern. Somehow, next to Fern and dressed as Kitty McLister, it was easier to feel confident. As they walked, they got some thumbs up from other girls (plus, a fair few *what-are-you-wearing stares*). And when they passed Mira's friend Bella, she shouted, 'Nice beret!'

'Glad you're giving gym skirts the comeback treatment,' said Mrs Lane, approvingly. 'Can't stand those sports leggings. Let your legs go free!'

Fern did some high kicks.

'And the beret deserves a shout-out,' said Mrs Lane.

Cassie felt a flutter of nerves. 'Is it honestly OK if I borrow it? I'll wash it and return it, I promise,' Cassie said quickly.

'To whom though? The girl it belonged to was here decades ago and she'd probably think it's hilarious you want to wear it. I know I do! Why don't you keep it?'

'Really?' Cassie felt like a frothy bottle of lemonade had opened in her chest. An original Pipson beret! She couldn't quite believe it. 'Thank you! I promise you I'll look after it, and I'll love it for ever, and—'

'I'm not that girl, by the way!' said Mrs Lane, sharply. 'I'm not that old.'

Fern laughed. 'Please may we borrow the key again tomorrow?'

'And what are you planning to forget tomorrow?'

'Nothing, honestly. But like you said, it's a dusty old mess in the stockroom, and it doesn't have to be.'

Cassie nodded enthusiastically. 'We could sort it out

as a way of saying thank you for the beret and the loan of the gym skirts. We could put things in piles. Clear it all up . . . There's some amazing stuff in there and—'

Mrs Lane put her hand up. 'Say no more. It's a yes from me.'

Cassie and Fern were still grinning when they flew through the doors and threw their bags on the benches.

Everyone had already headed to the basketball court. Cassie carefully tucked her beret into her bag. 'Are you coming?'

'I'll catch you up,' said Fern. She pulled out a sheet of stickers. Everyone's jumpers were lying around on the benches or hanging from the pegs. 'I'm going to stick a load of these on when no one's watching.'

'I'm not sure that's a good idea.' *In fact, I'm certain it's not*, thought Cassie.

'I think I need to put them on actual jumpers, so people really make the connection.'

'Are you sure people don't?' Cassie tried to make her

voice sound light. 'Only, this morning in form, Bea said that you tell her she's wearing fish food every thirty seconds!'

'Fish can swallow a lot of fibres in thirty seconds!'

'Good point.' Cassie quickly tucked Azra's jumper out of sight, under her coat. 'See you out there.'

An hour later, and Cassie was feeling better. It had been an OK match: and she flew around the court in her flippy gym skirt. Even Holly and Bea looked impressed. When Jules asked her where she'd got it, Cassie said it was a Pipson Original. It wasn't a lie – she told everyone it was from Lost Property – but the rebranding made it sound better.

Jules had laughed. 'Pipson Original? That's cool!'

Azra had been cool too, but in a different way. She'd fixed Cassie with a chilly stare as soon as she arrived and was still being off at the end of the match. Azra and Cassie were asked to carry the basketballs back to the equipment room, which meant they were last back to the changing rooms – which is where it was all kicking off. They could hear the scream as they turned the corner.

Holly was standing beside the door, her heirloom jumper in one hand, the Fish Food sticker in the other, and a hole in the fabric where she'd ripped the sticker off.

Chapter 9

'Who DID THIS?' she yelled.

'OMG! The stickers! Was it the stickers?' cried Azra. She was panicking like mad, her curls flying. 'Oh help, I knew this was a crime and now I'm part of a team that—'

'This was you?' Holly whipped her jumper through in the air. It nearly hit Azra.

Azra jumped like she'd got a massive static shock.

'You wrecked my jumper?'

'It wasn't Azra's fault!' Fern raced over. She had her jumper halfway over her head. She was stumbling around. Finally, she pulled her top off. 'It was me, Holly. I'm so sorry! I put a fish food sticker on it so people would make the connection between—'

'Between you and criminal damage?' Holly's eyes were flashing and darting around.

'This isn't putting a sticker on a teacher's book or on a mirror in the loos,' said Bea. She looked shaken. 'This is someone's property! This is Holly's. Actual. Jumper.'

'And you've broken it!' Holly held up her sweater like it was a piece of evidence.

The atmosphere was charged with tension. Everyone was dressed and ready to go, but most people were hanging around in the doorway watching the scene.

'My personal space has been invaded!' said Holly, pointing towards the part of the bench she'd got changed beside. 'It's sickening!'

'Like I said, I'm really sorry!' Fern's cheeks were hot. She looked like she was going to cry. She held out her own jumper. 'Have this for now, and I'll find you another one.'

Bea shook her head. 'This is not a replaceable jumper.'

'Too right it's not!' said Holly. She strutted the room, eyes darting. 'You think that your homemade sweater

– that by the way, Fern, looks like something you made in Infants – could EVER replace my beautiful vintage jumper that was passed on to me by my cousin?'

Fern's eyes went shiny with tears. 'No, of course not.'

Bea glared. 'You'll pay for this.'

'Only she CAN'T PAY!' said Holly. 'Because jumpers like mine can't even be bought!'

Azra threw herself down on the bench along the wall of the changing room. She stared at Cassie. 'No one is going to vote for our uniform design if Fern wrecks people's clothes . . .'

Cassie flashed a look at Azra. 'That's not important right now, Az.'

'And that drop in popularity is really going to cost us!' said Azra.

'I never meant to ruin your lovely jumper. I only wanted to help the fish because of all the tiny fibres.' Fern's voice was shaking.

Holly sliced the air above her head with her hand. 'I've had it up to here with you and the fish!'

'You don't even know these fish,' said Bea. 'It's not like they're your pets or something.'

Jules made a sympathetic face at Fern and began to scroll her phone.

'Not now Jules!' said Azra, looking so sick she was about to throw up. 'This is not a moment for comedy cats.'

Jules shoved the phone in her pocket.

'What actually happened?' Cassie tried to keep her voice steady.

'It's obvious what happened!' Holly's eyes were popping. 'I removed a sticker that had been put on my personal belongings without my permission. And the glue stuck to the sleeve, like—'

'Like glue!' said Bea, the tension bristling off her.

'Yeah! Like glue that's not supposed to be on a jumper. So when I pulled it off, naturally it ripped.' Holly mimed doing a massive tear in the air. 'And now!' She dangled the jumper from her fist. 'UNWEARABLE.'

Cassie looked at the damage on the sleeve. The hole

was tiny. Like a moth had taken a bite.

'I'll find you another one,' Fern was saying. She waved her jumper in the direction of the Sports Hall. 'There might be one in—'

Cassie's stomach plunged. *Whatever you say, don't say Lost Property.*

'Lost Property,' said Fern.

Holly and Bea screamed.

'You've gone too far this time, Fern.' Holly pushed past the crowd in the doorway. 'This is so NOT cool. We're off to tell Ginty.'

'We don't want to do this but we've no choice,' said Bea, with satisfaction. 'You've wasted fashion.'

Holly swung her jumper between her fingers. 'This thing is going straight to landfill.'

Fern's eyes brimmed with tears. 'That's the last thing I want! But don't worry about reporting this yourselves.' Fern trudged towards the doorway, her feet dragging on the floor. 'Because I'll hand myself in.'

'I'd rather be there,' said Holly.

They headed off in the direction of Ms Ginty's office. Holly and Bea were sauntering along. Fern followed, like she was being led to her death.

Cassie's skin prickled with outrage. 'Wait!' she said, suddenly. 'I can get your jumper fixed! I know a place where they'll make it more stylish than ever.'

Holly stopped in her tracks.

Cassie felt a thrill of exhilaration. If anyone could fix the jumper it was Mrs Khalid, Allan, and the others. And if she did this, Fern wouldn't be in trouble with Ms Ginty, and Azra wouldn't freak out about Fern's drop in popularity. 'You know the place where I got my new headband? That's where I'll take your jumper. I'll look after it and—'

'You don't mean . . .' Azra leapt up from the bench. 'OMG! Are you going to take it to KW?'

Cassie nodded.

'Wow!' Azra grabbed Cassie's arm. 'So you asked your neighbours about it then? Could have filled me in! How come you can take your jumper there?'

'My neighbour sort of works with them, so—'

'OMG!' said Azra breathlessly. 'This is so cool! Cassie's neighbour *does* work in fashion. You're so lucky, Holly! Your jumper is going to be even more exceptional.'

There was a long pause.

Fern was still shuffling off down the corridor.

'Or you could just borrow one of our silly fluffy jumpers,' said Cassie.

A second later, Holly walked over and dropped her jumper into Cassie's hands. 'This had better not be a joke.'

Cassie was still trying to catch her breath later that evening. She was sitting on her bed. She'd put her gran's sixties' skirt on with a tee-shirt. She tried to feel a kick of confidence.

'This skirt,' she said aloud, as if she was a fashion historian doing a piece to camera. 'Whipped-up strawberry sundaes at the seaside in the 1960s.'

She got up and did a little shimmy. She hummed a

few beats of a tune that her gran loved singing. Cassie couldn't remember the words, but it was something about a hedgehog.

She threw her arms out theatrically. 'And this skirt has also been on stage with my mum when she was a drama student.' She did a bow and pretended to hear the applause. She paused for a minute. Then she caught sight of Holly's jumper sticking out of her school bag.

'And now, for its next act! This skirt is going to inspire me. Being in this skirt is going to help me work out what the—'

Her phone buzzed.

Cassie threw herself down on her bed. She'd been ignoring her phone since she got home. But the notifications were flashing like mad. She skipped through the ones from Azra asking for more info ASAP on the KW situ. Cassie sent back a few hearts. Then she scrolled on.

Fern: Thanks so much Cassie! I owe you BIG TIME. And I don't know what KW is but I'm so glad you do. That seemed to really make the difference with Holly and Bea xxxx

Cassie: No problem! But do you think the Fish Food campaign is done now? I just think everyone . . . has made the connection.

Fern: Definitely! Today was awful. I can't believe I destroyed a jumper when I'm trying to save fashion waste. I'm the worst climate fashion person ever.

Cassie: You didn't destroy it!!!! It's one tiny stupid hole. I'll fix it.

Fern: I promise I'll pay you back somehow Cassie.

Chapter 10

The rest of that week – the first in October – began with warm, sunshiney weather. After school, Cassie and Emily drank iced peach tea and tried to slide down the fire pole without their flip flops falling off. But the days quickly rolled into blasting autumn storms. Wind whipped the last of the apples off the trees, there was a smell of damp wood smoke, and it began to get dark before dinner.

Cassie sat in her room, wrapped in her dressing gown, sketching ideas for Holly's jumper. She doodled a little heart, which was cute but un-Holly-ish, and looked up cool visible mending tutorials, which showed how stitches in different colours could cover up a hole and elevate the piece into something unique.

She felt a wave of nerves every time she remembered that she'd promised to take it to a real fashion brand. *What was she thinking?*

The KnitWits were working flat out on the blue dress. And she wasn't even sure if she should go to the next meeting after how angry Mira was with her the other night. On the other hand, she'd had a go at sewing Holly's jumper, got the thread in a mess, and had to undo everything.

The strap she was crocheting for Emily's climbing bag was looking good, though. The wool was in Emily's favourite shade of red, and it was super strength. As Cassie pulled her crochet hook in and out, the line of crochet formed a dense, cylinder shape, which was ideal for a bag strap.

Somehow, crocheting, like knitting, came naturally. Now Cassie had got the hang of it, it was just a case of repeating it until the strap was long enough.

Cassie's eyes flicked from her bag of knitting in the corner of her room to Holly's jumper, which was hanging over the door, like a shadow. She felt worried every time she saw it. To make herself feel better, she put her twenties' dress on over her pyjama bottoms.

She twirled in front of her mirror.

'Make a statement wherever you go!' Cassie said, in her tour guide voice. She threw her feather boa around her neck, and clipped a shoe rose in her hair. 'Let your true self shine with a riot of texture, glistening metallics and explosions of feathers!'

There was a knock on the door.

Cassie threw herself on the bed.

Emily came in. 'No need to dress up for me! I know your true self.'

'Ha ha.' Cassie grabbed her crocheting.

'That looks difficult. How do you do that tiny stitch?'

'It's easier now I'm into it.'

Emily climbed up onto the windowsill. She looked around her. 'I love coming in here. There's always something to look at. My bedroom's so tidy and boring . . .'

'That's because you're so super organized you even

have filing systems for birthday cards, Em!'

Emily dangled her legs down. The window was one of the old fire station arch windows with a wide ledge, like a big stone shelf. Cassie used it to display her shoe collection.

She had a pair of pixie boots (genuine mid-eighties), ballet flats that Emily used to wear to parties, a lime platform sandal that she'd seen in a charity shop, and a delicate pair of silver heels with tiny diamante straps. Beside each shoe, Cassie had written a little note, like they were displayed in a fashion museum.

Emily picked up the sign beside the heels. 'Note the kitten-shaped heel and the sparkles typical of the era. Worn by the owners' mother for her wedding.' Emily laughed. 'Factually correct but sooooo hard to believe! These are the most un-Mum like shoes I can imagine.'

'I know! If we hadn't seen the photos, I'm not sure I'd believe Mum went clackety clack up the aisle!'

'Don't worry, she was back in her hiking boots for the honeymoon.'

'And a cagoule!' Cassie giggled. 'Who goes wild camping in Scotland for their holiday-of-a-lifetime?' She felt slightly bad. To be fair to Mum and Dad they looked so happy in those photos. Even though it had poured down the whole time. 'We shouldn't be so judgy, Em. We've got matching pyjamas!'

'Oh yes, the family pyjamas . . .'

'The coolest in town!' said Mum, barging into the room. She was wearing Adrenalyn-branded pyjama bottoms too.

'Thanks for knocking,' said Cassie. 'I appreciate the privacy and respect that you show me.'

Mum wandered over to what Cassie called Library Corner, where her books were piled up on the floor, with her jeans and jumper on top – like they were on a plinth. Mum picked up a fashion sketch that Cassie had done of a uniform, which was propped against it.

Cassie had drawn a Pipson beret, stars on the sleeves of the jumper, and a white blouse that billowed like clouds.

'Ooh, what's this?'

Cassie took the sketch away and threw it towards the end of the bed. 'Nothing!'

'Don't start without me!' said Dad.

'Start what?' Emily was trying on the platform sandal.

'The family meeting,' said Dad. He came into the room, carrying a tray of mugs, and he had a can of oat squirty cream under his arm.

'Great, we're having a family meeting in my bedroom. Just what I need, after the week I've had.' Cassie swept her crocheting to the side of the bed. She picked up Holly's jumper. She should probably concentrate on that once the others had cleared off.

'What sort of a week have you had?' said Mum. She was absentmindedly tidying Cassie's pencil crayons.

Where to start? Mira being mad at me, Holly wanting her jumper fixed, Azra kicking off because we don't have a uniform design yet . . . Cassie shrugged. 'Don't worry, I didn't fall off a cliff so you wouldn't be interested!'

'I'm glad to hear you're OK.'

OK? Is she joking?

Mum dropped a handful of pencils. She shoved them back into the pot. Cassie put Holly's jumper on her lap. It may be ripped but it was still warm. The evening was getting chilly.

Dad handed out hot chocolates.

He gave Emily the cream, and she squirted a load straight into her mouth.

Cassie took a sip. 'What's the meeting about? Because if it's about not putting the lid back on the toothpaste then it's not me.'

'It's lots more fun than that,' said Dad, running a hand through his hair. 'It's good news, really.'

'Not again,' said Cassie.

Dad put his mug down on the floor. 'We're running some new events. For families. It's all about getting parents, carers and their teens—'

'Teens?' said Emily, looking appalled.

'Everyone out there together. Climbing, hill walking, wild swimming, the usual stuff . . .'

Cassie blew the top of her hot chocolate.

Mum and Dad went on about how parents struggle to find cool activities that interest teens and how this could be a whole new area of business.

'It's called Family Adrenalyn!' said Dad. 'Mum came up with it,' he added, proudly.

'OK.' Emily gave Cassie a sideways look. 'I guess that means you'll be out a lot at weekends?'

'Which is perfectly fine!' said Cassie, quickly. 'Em and I can both cook dinner for when you get back.'

'Thanks girls,' said Dad, sincerely. He took a sip. A foamy moustache appeared on his upper lip. 'But—'

'Like we said, they're family events,' said Mum, firmly. 'This is about our family too. So . . . you both have to be there.'

WHAT? Cassie's insides were screaming.

'We're really busy right now,' began Emily. 'There's school, climbing, Cassie's got the KnitWits . . .'

'Well maybe . . .' said Cassie. She quickly shut up. She hadn't been sure if she should go to the KnitWits any more, now that Mira was mad at her. On the other hand, she needed help with Holly's jumper. And if it got her out of Family Adrenalyn . . .

Dad waved his hands. 'We've got some fantastic plans! Rope swings across the river! Rafting . . .' He went on, throwing out words like campfire, agility courses, teamwork and lunch.

Mum looked excited. 'An exciting, fun-filled, *family* day learning new skills, and the local riverbank in autumn—'

'Is spectacular,' finished Dad, with feeling. 'Like we said on the marketing for the event, it's such a photogenic place. Perfect for teens to do their social media posts!'

'Did you actually put that on the marketing?' Cassie licked the edge of her mug. Drips of chocolate were running down the sides.

Emily laughed.

Mum nodded. 'What could be a more incredible backdrop?'

*Erm, how about the costume department of a theatre,
inside vintage shops, dress exhibitions, medieval castles,
the Edwardian tea room at the museum, Georgian
ballrooms, Victorian art galleries . . .*

'The riverbank is lovely.' Emily picked up Mum's
wedding shoes. She did a tap-tap of the heels along the
windowsill. 'But like I said, we've got stuff to do.'

Cassie squirmed.

Mum shook her head. 'It's only one week, and we
need you.'

Dad laughed, lightly. 'How would it look if we couldn't
even get our own kids to join in?'

'Normal,' said Emily, amiably. 'You'll just look normal.
No teenager wants to spend a day like this with their
parents. And I say that as someone who LOVES outdoor
activities.'

'And your parents?' joked Mum.

Dad wiped his frothy milk moustache. 'To be honest . . .
that is kind of the problem we're hitting.'

'The thing is, we need numbers,' said Mum. 'We've

only had two families book so far, and one of them said they're not sure the kids will come. So what we were thinking is if you have any friends at school who'd like it, please invite them along!'

'Offer it to them for free,' said Dad. 'Obviously. We're just going to run this thing as a loss leader for now.'

Emily held her hand up. 'That's a no.'

Dad nodded slowly. 'OK, fair enough to not asking friends. We should have done better on the marketing.' He opened his hands. 'Our fault. But we do need you there to support us. This is a family business—'

'When is it again?' said Emily.

'A week tomorrow,' said Mum.

A week tomorrow was the day of the CommunKnitty awards, when the KnitWits would have to show the blue dress to the judges.

The only way Cassie could see her vision sewn into life was if she went to the KnitWits a week on Saturday. Cassie knew that she probably couldn't be the model, but she hadn't given up hope of going to see the dress in person.

She blew across the top of her hot chocolate. The cream circled the rim like foam washed up on the sea. 'I promise I'll come to Family Adrenalyn another time, but I just can't that day. I'm no good at climbing or rafting anyway. You're better off without me!'

'We love how you've thrown yourself into knitting—' said Mum. 'But you're going to have to miss it—'

'Thrown myself into knitting? You literally forced me to go to the KnitWits! And now you're saying I have to miss it—'

Dad pulled a sympathetic face. 'It's only one week, Cas!'

Cassie held up Emily's bag strap. 'This is important too! I'm making a bag strap using a super-strong stitch that I've learnt. That's every bit as skilled as doing rope knots on a raft . . .'

'Agreed!' said Mum. 'We definitely need you on the river now.' She went to give Cassie a friendly nudge, but Mum moved too quickly on the bed and it was more of a shove than a nudge.

'Arghhhhh!' Cassie screamed. A large slop of hot chocolate had spilt onto Holly's jumper. 'OMG! MUM!'

'Sorry,' said Mum.

The stain was rapidly spreading across the top. 'You've gone and made it worse when I'm meant to be making it better! This is a disaster!'

'It's only a bit of hot chocolate,' said Dad, though he looked worried.

'That's gone all over the jumper! OMG!' Cassie's heart pounded.

'Calm down,' said Mum, sharply. 'It was an accident.'

Within seconds Cassie was in the bathroom, throwing the jumper into the sink. She put both taps on full. Her insides felt like mush. Emily came in and handed her a towel.

'I'll need to wring it out first,' said Cassie.

'I meant for your face,' said Emily.

Cassie wiped her tears. 'On the bright side, at least I don't have to go to stupid Family Adrenalyn,' said Cassie, with feeling. 'I've tried to fix the hole in the jumper myself, but there's no way I can cover up the stains as well. I've not got the skills. I *have* to go back to the KnitWits.'

'Well go this week then,' said Dad, in a calm voice. 'And sort out the jumper, and remember Family Adrenalyn isn't until the week after.'

'And if I'm going to the KnitWits tomorrow, then I'm going next week too and seeing the dress in real life. I don't want to get so close to seeing it and then not be there for the real thing,'

'We're a team, remember,' said Dad.

'Count me out of the team for this one.'

Mum shook her head. 'Cassie!' she said firmly 'You're twelve years old. If we say you're coming on a family activity day, then you're coming on a family activity day.'

The second they were gone, Cassie exploded. 'They're so annoying! And confusing. One minute I have to go to the KnitWits, the next I'm not allowed to—'

'I agree,' said Emily. 'You go to the KnitWits if you want but I'll *have* to do it. I don't think we have a choice. Like Dad says, we're a team! Anyway, what if we didn't go and Family Adrenalyn is a disaster?'

'Yes, but what if it's a success?'

'You're right,' said Emily, thoughtfully. 'They'll want to run it again and again . . .'

'Exactly. And before we know it, someone at school will hear about it and be dragged along there by their parents—'

Emily covered her face with her hands. 'Stop it! I know where there's a new packet of Jammie Dodgers. I bet I can slide down the fire pole faster than you can eat one. And then you can try!'

Cassie shook her head. 'Thanks, Em.' She picked up the wool and needle. 'But *this* is what my knitty brain needs right now.'

Chapter 11

The KnitWits session was in full swing when Cassie opened the door of the community centre. As soon as she arrived, she could feel the blue dress buzz.

Milo waved her over. His fringe looked floppier than usual, with the sweat of rushing around getting things ready. Cassie could just about see his eyes. 'Serena and Leta are finishing the cuffs of the sleeves—'

They were in front of machines, sewing like they were under exam conditions.

'Allan's embroidered the sleeves that the others are finishing, and he's now cutting out the lining.' Milo pointed to the corner, where Allan was laying fabric out on the table.

It was blue satin. He'd cut off the spaghetti straps

and was doing some measurements.

'It used to be a nightdress, apparently,' laughed Milo. 'Ideal for the lining because it's not too light or dark to show through anywhere.

'It's so pretty!' Cassie ran her fingers over it. She told herself not to get attached to the dress. But it was hard when even the inside layer was perfect.

She watched as Allan scribbled numbers on a piece of paper. Finally, he finished his calculations. Then he threw away the tape measure and picked up the scissors.

Cassie picked up one of the straps from the pile of scraps. She twisted it. 'Fingers crossed,' she said, excitedly.

'No need to cross your fingers if you've done the Maths,' Allan said, in his trademark deep voice. 'But until we know who will be modelling it, we'll have to make everything as adjustable and flexible as we can.'

'If all else fails, I'll do it myself,' said Milo. 'But I'm not keen and there's no way I'll fit the silver trainers.' He looked at his clumpy work boots.

'Leta says her niece might do it,' said Allan. 'But it's not ideal as she's not properly part of the group. She's going to speak to her later.'

Cassie kept her eyes down. She felt like she had the words *I Want to Be the Girl in the Blue Dress with the Silver Trainers* stamped on her forehead.

Milo explained how they were putting ribbons in at the back to make the bodice adjustable, and the waistline of the skirt could be altered. 'And the sleeves are so oversized, we could hide a cat or a small dog in there,' he laughed.

Jules would love that, thought Cassie. *She'd be able to take Bevan to school if they designed billowing sleeves for the uniform.* The thought of school made her stomach flip. She had Holly's jumper stuffed into her bag. But everyone seemed so busy she didn't dare ask for help with it.

A minute later, and Allan had cut confidently along the lines. He threw the lining over to Milo. A shot of cobalt blue flying through the air.

'Your fringe next,' said Allan, theatrically. He snapped the scissors in the air towards Milo. 'One, two, three, GONE!'

Milo dashed off to the sewing machine. Cassie took a deep breath and went over to where Mrs Khalid and Mira were sitting.

Mrs Khalid was knitting a piece of the cuff to add to the statement sleeves on the dress. Mira had an A3 piece of paper and was sticking on pieces of fabric and writing notes.

Mrs Khalid smiled. 'Good to see you, Cassie.' She clicked her knitting needles together.

'That looks cool,' Cassie said. She pointed to the paper.

'Mira's explaining the creative process behind the blue dress,' said Mrs Khalid. 'She's doing the competition entry for her Art project about recycling fabric. How great is that?'

'Really great,' said Cassie.

Mira flashed her eyes. 'By the way, for the purposes

of school I've told everyone it's a fictionalized piece.'

Cassie nodded, quickly. 'I get it.'

'Because it's best not to write things down when it comes to the competition,' Mira said, pointedly.

Cassie flushed deeply. Mira must have seen what she'd written in Mrs Khalid's flat. She should have made sure her scrap of paper was put in the bin. 'Understood.'

Mira went on. 'This is pure fantasy, not based in reality—'

Mrs Khalid laughed. 'I agree, this place is like a dream!'

Mira looked up at Cassie for a second and smiled.

A second later, Mira was back to her sketching, and Mrs Khalid's knitting needles were clicking away. Cassie looked around her. Everyone was busy, and no one seemed to need any help.

And there was no way she could ask for advice about Holly's jumper either.

The idea of facing Holly on Monday without her jumper being restored to its former glory had given Cassie a fitful sleep. But she should have known the

KnitWits would be immersed in the blue dress.

Even so, it felt awkward to just leave.

After a minute or so, Mrs Khalid cleared her throat. She didn't speak but her eyes flicked in the direction of the kitchen.

Cassie smiled in relief. 'Shall I put the kettle on?'

There was something about holding a warm drink that made people more friendly, thought Cassie. Once Mira's hands were around the cup of tea Cassie gave her, she instantly seemed calmer and more relaxed.

'This is so beautiful!' Cassie ran her fingers gently over the final stitches of the shrug.

'Thank you!' Mrs Khalid said brightly. 'Mira did lots of it.'

'I'm not very good at it,' said Mira. 'My stitches had to be redone at some points.'

'It's easy to make mistakes when you're knitting. As long as you never make them with the tea.' Mrs Khalid lifted up her mug. 'Lovely cup, thank you, Cassie.'

Mira smiled. 'My nani has priorities!'

Cassie felt a glow spreading through her. She listened while Mrs Khalid explained how her family never threw out old fabric or clothes – dresses were passed on, for example, or made into skirts, tops, children's clothes, cushion covers or even pretty napkins. 'And if all else fails, they're made into dishcloths.'

'You must have some very high-end dishcloths,' said Cassie. Mrs Khalid's clothes were always beautifully made and worn without a single crease or fraying hem.

'Yeah, top quality!' Mira rolled her eyes at her grandmother. 'I cleaned the pans last night with a piece of old ballgown, didn't I?'

'Samira!' Mrs Khalid pointed to the paper. 'You've missed out the embroidery on the sleeves.'

Mira grabbed her pencil.

A sparkle went through Cassie's brain. 'That's just like the Tudors, isn't it?'

Her fashion history book had a section about how clothes were passed on in Court all the time, and how some of them were still around today. 'Do you know there's a piece of fabric called the Bacton Altar Cloth that still exists and it's part of a long-lost skirt that belonged to Elizabeth I!'

After a minute or two, Mrs Khalid put a box on the table and lifted the lid. 'Talking of old things, I've brought my silver trainers.'

Cassie nearly fell off her chair. The silver trainers had been under the table this whole time? She felt her breath catch in her throat. UNBOXING ALERT!

Everyone gathered around.

'Leta, you'll know more about the background of the trainers,' said Mrs Khalid as she took off the lid.

'Not really my area but—' said Leta. She began to whizz through the history of trainers, and how Mrs Khalid's pair was one of the first fashion pairs to hit the UK. 'Back then, in the late sixties, we were only just starting to say the word trainer, instead of training shoe.'

'I saved up everything to get them,' said Mrs Khalid.

'I remember the day I went to buy them. And how I wore them home, and danced out of the shop.' She pulled back the tissue paper.

Cassie was leaning on the table, her nose practically touching the box. She was alight with excitement.

Out came the super-rare silver sports shoes, with the brand's signature stripes down the side, in a dazzling cerulean blue.

Mrs Khalid held them out. 'Go on, try them on, Cassie!'

Cassie was trembling as her hands touched the shoes. 'Really?' She didn't dare look at Mira. But there was no way she could turn down this chance to try a pair of trainers so old they were iconic.

They slipped onto her feet as if they'd been handmade for her. The fabric was soft as butter. She carefully pulled the laces together, and tied a bow. They felt almost too precious to wear.

She tapped her feet on the floor. Mrs Khalid gave her a clap.

Milo shouted from across the room, 'The shoe fits!'

Cassie laughed. She could understand how Mrs Khalid had once danced out of a shop in these shoes.

Then she caught Mira's eyes, watching her warily. Cassie blushed. She slipped the trainers off and put them back in the box, as gently as if they were a puppy.

'OK,' said Leta. 'Back to work!'

'Do you need us?' said Mira. She had finished her Art sketches.

'I'll let you know if we do,' said Mrs Khalid. 'But feel free to start a new project! I'm sure you can think of something creative.'

Mira scooped up a fistful of fabric scraps from the table. She showered them down again, like brightly coloured sweets. She shrugged at Cassie. 'Got any ideas?'

Ten minutes later, and they had a plan for Holly's jumper. Mira said Cassie was right that just mending the hole was a bad idea. They didn't have the sewing skills to do cool visible mending or invisible stitches.

And anyway, there was also the problem of the hot chocolate stains to deal with. Mira said the only way forward was patches.

They hit the haberdashery table. They ran their fingers through ribbons, wrapped realms of fabric around themselves, and tipped out an old biscuit tin that was full of buttons, cut-out hearts, beads, bows, flowers and jewels. Everything had been kept from past projects and clothes.

'Wow! There are so many things.' Cassie picked up a vintage blue and cream button. 'I wonder where this came from?'

Mira shrugged. 'Who knows?' She picked up a silver bead. 'My nani says there is a thing here for every project and there's a project here for every thing!'

Cassie lifted up a felt badge in the shape of a welly. She raised her eyebrow. 'Even this?'

'I made that when I was little!' Mira looked annoyed.

'It's lovely, honestly I was only—'

'Joking,' said Mira. 'Calm down, I was joking. The welly

is horrible!' Mira held up a fistful of stars. 'These, though
–' they were already stitched along the edges, had
been cut out of what looked like an old jumper, and
were soft as marshmallows and pale as early spring sky –
'. . . are gorgeous. What do you think?'

'Yes, please! They're amazing!'

Mira laid one over the rip in Holly's sleeve. Then
she scattered others, in the same pattern as the stars
on her Taylor Swift cardigan. 'School uniform, Taylor's
Version?'

'Mira's Version!' said Cassie.

'Mira and Cassie's version,' said Mira.

They both laughed.

'Wow! She's going to love it.' Cassie got a reel of
thread. She narrowed her eyes to get it through the
needle.

'Wait, you mean this isn't your jumper?' Mira looked
confused.

'Sorry, I thought I'd said . . .'

Cassie explained about the Fish Food Fiasco and

about Fern having to hand herself in to Ms Ginty if the jumper wasn't fixed, and because Mira was nodding and grimacing in all the right places, she told her how anxious she felt being in the same form as Holly and Bea.

'Thanks for listening, by the way,' she said. Something about the way they were working side by side stitching the stars made it easier to talk.

Mira stabbed her needle into a star. 'People like this Holly girl are the exact reason I don't tell anyone about the KnitWits. Urghh! I hate how judgy and mean some people are at school.'

'Same.'

Mira looked angry. 'If anyone laughed at the KnitWits or, even worse, was mean about my nani, it would be awful. I feel the same about Leta, Milo and the others. Even Allan, really.'

Cassie nodded. 'And the annoying thing is, we're making her jumper iconic now, with the stars—'

'Not! Like! That!' said Allan, in a booming voice. He was

suddenly there at the table. 'You can't use embroidery thread on a fabric like that jumper.'

Cassie jumped in shock. 'Sorry, that was me!'

'And as for the spacing! Haven't you heard of a ruler?'

Cassie and Mira exchanged glances.

Allan shook his head. 'Don't move.'

Two minutes later, and he was back. 'This thread is the only one that's fine enough for the job. I know it's purple, is that a problem?'

'The colour's fine!' said Cassie, quickly.

'But before you sew them on you need to stitch up the actual hole,' Allan said. He shook his head, as if this was something even a toddler could get right. He put an orange inside the jumper, to help him see where the hole was.

A few stitches later and no one could see the hole, anyway. Then he attached a blue star in seconds.

'Wow!' breathed Cassie. 'How do you do that?'

'Magic needles,' said Allan throatily.

Mira laughed.

'Otherwise known as experience,' Allan said, like he was projecting his voice across an auditorium. 'Time and patience.'

'It's not that easy for us, Allan,' said Mira. 'We haven't got all of those things.'

'But you've both made Monday a lot easier for me. Honestly, you've saved my life,' said Cassie. *More than you know.* As long as Holly liked these stars and no one found out what KW stands for . . .

'Team work!' said Mira.

Cassie grinned. 'I mean it, though. Thanks a zillion.'

Allan rolled his eyes. 'Tell me you know that's not a real number?'

'We need someone to model the skirt!' shouted Milo, from across the room.

'I've asked my niece. The one who's an Art student,' said Leta. 'She loves the idea of all the blues! But she's not sure she's free next weekend.'

'We really need someone *now* so we can get this properly fitted,' said Milo, sounding frustrated. 'Come on, guys. Anyone not working on the blue dress?'

Allan waved his hand. 'These two are free.'

'Sorry!' Mira pulled the tape measure between her hands. 'I'm measuring stars and mending a jumper to save Cassie's life. And I've told you, I can't be the model anyway. I'm basically ideologically opposed to the whole concept of using women as models.'

'Cassie?' said Allan, impatiently. 'Is it also against your principles to try on a beautifully designed, competition-worthy, CommunKnitty blue dress?'

Cassie's cheeks went hot. She put her head down and carefully put a needle into a felt star.

Milo was waving the midnights skirt. The finely knitted overlayer, with pearls and flowers shimmered like frothy clouds at dusk. He shouted over, 'Wool you be a pal and come and try this on for us?'

Cassie grabbed her phone. 'OMG! I didn't realize it was so late! I've got to go.' She looked at Allan. 'I'm so sorry, I can't try the dress on! Thanks for the massive help with the jumper.' She packed it away.

Allan looked annoyed. 'If push comes to shove, I'll be the model next week, but it would be a lot better if you did it. Apart from anything else, Cassie, you're the one who fits the vintage trainers.'

'I'm sorry! I've just got to rush.' Cassie nearly ran out of the hall. 'Thanks again for all the help, Mira! And you too Allan.'

It was Monday morning, and Azra was shrieking. 'You have more than delivered!' She stroked the sleeve of Holly's jumper. 'Look at those stars. Hollywood vibes! Oh my gosh, Cassie. KW is THE BEST.'

Cassie's stomach squirmed. 'You are way too much excitement for a Monday morning, Azra.'

'It's wild!' said Fern. 'So beautiful.' She impulsively threw her arms around Cassie. Cassie's beret was knocked sideways. She looked at the stitching on Holly's jumper. 'I didn't know you could sew, Cassie.'

'I'm only learning.'

'But *you* didn't do this, wasn't it KW?' said Azra.

'Hmm.' Cassie pretended to find a stray thread on the jumper. A second later, Holly and Bea stormed into 7B's form room.

'Got it?' said Holly.

'Of course.' Cassie's nerves fluttered. There was a hushed silence. A few of the other girls had come over to see the jumper.

Cassie held her breath as Holly examined the jumper like she was a forensic scientist. She pulled the sleeve where the first star was and turned it inside out to look for the hole, like she was trying to find evidence from the scene of the crime. At one point, she traced the shape of the star that Allan had done. 'Cool,' said Holly slowly.

'And mathematically correct!' said Cassie.

Finally, Holly slipped the jumper over her head. It fitted snugly and perfectly over her white shirt, and the starry sleeves instantly elevated the outfit.

'Wow!' broke in Jules. 'This is the best jumper Pipson High has ever seen.'

Azra turned to Holly. 'Do you love the jumper? Not just as a person, I mean, but as one of the coordinators?' said Azra. She had her pen poised over her notebook.

Holly put her shoulders back. 'I appreciate how it's a designer piece, and not from the stupid school uniform shop.'

Cassie squirmed. 'More like mended, really? Or re-fashioned from an unknown brand . . .'

'An up-and-coming brand,' said Azra quickly. 'Which is about to get really well known.'

Holly shook her hair. 'And as a person, I love it. It's just so . . . me!'

'And you won't go to Ms Ginty,' said Cassie, feeling relieved.

'Why would I go to Ginty?'

'No reason! It's just you—' *threatened Fern with that exact thing on Friday.*

'I was never going to go to Ginty.' Holly did a massive eye roll. 'You guys are such babies.'

*

The news soon whipped around that Holly had a starry jumper. Mainly the publicity came from Holly herself. She sat stroking the stars in every lesson and in the canteen queue she talked about how iconic it was.

'One of a kind,' Holly announced loudly, as everyone was lining up for food.

'A Holly kind,' said Bea.

Cassie tried to ignore them.

Holly had already massively wound her up during History. The lesson was about symbols of power during the Elizabethan age. The teacher had talked about how only people in the royal family were allowed to wear purple.

Cassie had put her hand up. She wanted to tell everyone how this was because the colour of the dye was rare and expensive, so it was a way of showing power and wealth.

But Holly had shouted out about how the stars on her sleeve had purple stitches, which showed her elite status. The teacher had given Holly an achievement point.

Cassie took a deep breath. *Forget Holly*, she told herself. As long as she's not going on about KW, it's not a problem. She looked ahead to the counter. *Shall I have veggie burritos or cherry tomato spaghetti?*

'And the thing is, stars really match my personality!' said Holly, loudly.

A few girls in the queue beside them looked at the stars. Cassie couldn't hear what they were saying, but they there were nodding and smiling.

'This is what I call school jumpers: Holly's Version!'

This time Holly was so loud that Mira, sitting at a table nearby with Bella, looked up. Cassie held her breath. But Holly seemed so focused on attention from everyone in the queue, she didn't even clock that Mira was there.

Cassie gave Mira a sideways glance. Mira's eyes were dancing. Cassie wished she could say *Allan's Version, actually*, because Holly was showing everyone the mathematically correct star.

Mira crossed her fingers over, in a little KW sign. She

made it look as if she was pulling a piece of spaghetti off her fork. Cassie felt a glow of warmth.

'Holly loves it!' squealed Azra. 'This is so-ooo good for us, Cassie. We're already proving we can design a uniform that one of the judges really likes.' She dropped her voice. 'Or KW is, anyway.'

'That's so true,' said Fern, who was behind them in the queue. She tapped Cassie on the arm. 'You know what? Maybe we should do stars-on-sleeves for our uniform design?'

Azra clapped her hands. 'OMG! Yes, because Holly already loves them!'

Holly did a little shimmy of her shoulders. 'You can't click the buy button on a jumper like this. This has been specially designed just for Holly.'

'Just for you,' said Bea.

Fern did an exaggerated impression of Holly wiggling her shoulders. 'I love the way she's showing it off! It'll mean everyone will want jumpers with big starry sleeves and then, boom!' She threw out her hands like an explosion. 'We will deliver.'

'And win!' said Azra, breathlessly. 'Oversized, decorative sleeves are so on trend.'

Cassie laughed. 'Like they were in the Renaissance. Do you know back then, lots of the extreme, ornate sleeves were detachable, and passed down the generations?'

Fern did a double thumbs up. 'Sounds very eco. I'll look out for some material that would otherwise be wasted. Maybe in Lost Property? We can make a prototype.'

'History, and stinky old jumpers aside,' Azra's fringe was flipping up with excitement, 'this idea could actually work. Holly will love it because it'll be like she started the trend, and now everyone will be able to wear a jumper like hers.'

Fern looked confused. 'Surely that's the bit she *won't* like, Azra.'

'Everyone gets to vote on their favourite design, not just Holly.' Cassie's mind raced. If they used oversized sleeves with stars as part of their uniform design, then people would associate them with it. And if they did that, it would put them in a great position to win the uniform redesign and it would also take the jumper one step further away from KW . . .

They were at the front of the queue now. Holly and Bea were already sitting down. Holly was holding her burrito at an awkward angle so that the stars were still on show.

A minute later, Cassie, Fern and Azra were at a table next to the window, and were talking about whether a skirt, skort or pair of trousers would work best with starry sleeves.

'Ooh.' Azra's phone buzzed with a notification. She pointed a potato wedge at her screen. 'Holly's posted a story to promote her jumper on the year seven chat.'

Cassie stopped, a forkful of pasta halfway to her mouth.

'There are photos of her sleeves, and a little caption,' said Azra.

It was only the year seven group chat, Cassie told

herself quickly. Year eleven students like Mira weren't on it. But Emily had warned her posts got copied and forwarded, and before you knew it, went right round the school.

Azra wiped her hands. 'I'll read it out.'

> **Holly: My iconic jumper! Refashioned and super styled by a totally new fashion label called KW. You heard it here first.**

'These stars! Is it true that they were done by a new fashion brand?' Ms Ginty stopped 7B on their way to Maths. 'I've heard the rumours, but I'd love to see the stars for myself.'

Cassie's insides squirmed as Ms Ginty peered at Holly's jumper. Holly held her sleeves out. 'That's right, they were exclusively made for me.'

'Wow!' She smiled at the whole class. 'You can't go wrong with celestial embellishments! And they certainly look professionally done.'

'They were, Miss.' Holly shot a sideways glance at Cassie. 'At an up-and-coming brand.' She looked unsure of herself. 'It's quite small and new?'

Cassie nervously rubbed the fabric of her cuff between her finger and thumb.

'Well, you're very lucky.' Ms Ginty smiled. 'I doubt the brand will stay small for long if they can transform an ordinary old school jumper into such a beautiful piece.'

Holly looked super annoyed.

'And oversized, super sleeves are really in right now,' said Azra. She was suddenly at the front of the crowd, and next to Holly. 'So, Cassie and Fern and I – you know the first fashion team?'

Ms Ginty nodded.

'We're thinking about doing the stars on sleeves for our uniform design, too,' Azra said.

Holly looked furious.

'Or butterflies and hearts!' Azra said, in a panicky voice. 'Sorry, Holly, it's just everyone really loves it and it's not like you did it yourself—'

'This jumper is my version,' Holly pretended to smile politely in front of Ms Ginty. 'You can't create a fake version. That's against the rules.'

'And it's called cheating,' said Bea.

'It's not,' said Fern. 'The sleeves are great, but the design itself isn't new, is it Cassie?'

Azra turned to Cassie. 'Didn't you say statement sleeves have been around for ages?'

An image of Elizabeth I in her battle-fresh Armada portrait flew into Cassie's mind. Opulent, extravagant and powerful, that dress was the best example ever of dream sleeves. She shifted from one foot to the other. 'Something like that, yes.'

Jules was waving a photo on her phone. 'If it makes you feel better, stars are loads of things! My cat had this collar . . . hang on . . . I'll play you the clip, because the stars on it made a jangly noise.'

'Great! Now we're going to be styled like cats,' said Holly, angrily. 'I think designing clothes for animals is against the rules too.'

Ms Ginty laughed. 'This is our school, our rules!' She swished off down the corridor, in a pair of floaty culottes that rippled like water. 'And the main rule is to have fun with this project!'

'No pressure or anything,' said Mr Jackson, at registration the next day. 'But I've made a bet. No money involved. But it's with Mrs Upta.' Mrs Upta was a Chemistry teacher, whose classroom was next door. 'It's about whose form is going to win the uniform redesign competition. Anyway, you're such a talented bunch, that I've said a group in 7B will win!'

'We will!' said Azra.

Others were shouting out too:

'We've designed a jumpsuit!'

'You should see our sweatshirt.'

Azra flashed Cassie an excited look. 'But we've got the KW starry sleeves that everyone already loves!'

A few of the others were saying they'd already finished their designs. Jules had designed one with a pocket for cat treats, a group of girls who cycled to school had done a sporty design with leggings and hoodies.

'We've got to get a move on,' said Azra. 'All designs have to be in on Monday. We have to meet up on Saturday morning, and get it done.'

'Saturday's hard because . . . *I'm off to see the Blue Dress with the Silver Trainers.*

Cassie didn't want to mention KW again. Azra was already obsessed with it. 'I told you Mum and Dad are running that family adventure day, so . . .'

'We have to win this thing!'

Fern leant over. 'I don't care about winning—'

Azra rolled her eyes. 'Not this again. I thought you'd got into the competition now?'

Fern smiled. She lifted up a canvas bag and tipped out a load of old uniform onto her lap. 'But I think we need to use it to highlight a better, climate-friendly way to dress. Anyway, I went to Lost Property on my way in.' She held up a knitted tank circa mid-eighties.

'Lovely!' Cassie reached over and felt the wool. 'Tanks are a great foundation piece. We could style it with wide-leg trousers for autumn or a sarong in summer, or over a shirt so you get to see the starry sleeves . . .'

Azra looked interested. 'OK, but we do have to make decisions and get our entry in on time!'

Fern bounced the clothes on her lap. 'More where that came from!' She held up a handful of shirts, a long pleated skirt and a pair of leg warmers.

She explained how she'd been back to see Mrs Lane, who said she could take as much vintage uniform as she wanted, and in return, Fern had offered to tidy up the stockroom during her lunchtimes.

'I can meet you in town on Saturday?' Fern stuffed the skirts and tops back into the bag. 'All we need to do is one sketch, and we can just cut some of this fabric up and glue together our design.'

Azra's nose wrinkled up. 'That sounds a bit . . . homemade. We need to make sure this looks pro.' She looked over to where a few of the other groups were checking designs on their phones.

'Make sure you get those entries done on time and bring home the win for 7B,' smiled Mr Jackson. 'Because if I lose this bet, I'm the one who has to have an ice bucket poured over me at the school autumn fayre.'

Chapter 12

Cassie and Azra were walking through the school gates. It was the end of the day. Holly and Bea had raced off the second the bell went, got hot fruit lattes from the cafe on the corner, and were parading them in front of everyone.

'Got the last of the blueberry and vanilla whip, by the way!' said Bea. She stopped in front of Cassie and Azra. 'And Holly got almond raspberry chai.'

Holly held her creamy pink drink next to her face, and took a selfie. 'Only the best for the girl with the genuine KW sweater. The only one-off and not a fake!'

Cassie rolled her eyes at Azra. 'Excuse me,' she said to Holly. 'I need to get past.'

'Hang on,' said Holly. She was looking at her phone.

'You OK?' said Bea. She blew on the top of her drink. 'You look a bit shocked.'

'You know I messaged my mum about how I'd accidentally burned a hole in my skirt during Chemistry?'

Bea nodded. It was only a tiny hole. But everyone had been given a massive warning about sticking to the safety rules during Science. Holly had been sent to the loos to take off her skirt, and put on her PE leggings.

Holly looked rattled. 'Well, she won't buy me a new one! And I've only got one of the skirts I like. There's no way I'm wearing the other one that Mum got.' She made a face at Bea. 'The pleated one.'

'You can't, Hols.' Bea swallowed. 'It's practically a midi.'

Azra's diamante notebook sparkled in the afternoon light. She pulled out a pen. 'You don't like midi skirts? Okaaay. What do you think of skorts?'

'Not now, Azra,' said Cassie. She flashed her eyes. 'I'm sorry about your skirt . . . situation, but I've got to get to the bus stop, so if you don't mind—'

'I do mind.' Holly blocked her way.

Cassie tried to make her voice sound light. 'Well, I'm not going to take my skirt off now and hand it over. So I don't know what—'

'I know what you can do.' Holly juggled her cup in one hand, and pulled out her skirt from her bag. It had been PE last thing so she'd kept her leggings on. 'Take this and make it exceptional, like my starry-sleeved sweater!'

'That was a one-off,' said Cassie. 'Sorry, but I don't have time!' – *to be your personal seamstress.*

Azra's eyes darted to Cassie.

Holly looked at Azra. 'I know you're trying to copy what I've got here, and that's a little bit of a cheat, no matter what Ginty says. But how about this for a deal? If you get KW to do my skirt, I'll let you use the starry sleeves for your uniform design.'

Cassie nearly laughed. *Wow, thanks! So, you own the design rights now?*

'I'll showcase it,' Holly said, airily. 'And as a

coordinator—'

Azra bit her lip. 'She's right, Cassie, this could be good for the competition.'

'I'm not going to see my contact from KW this week anyway. I've told you I've got that . . . family day.'

Cassie wasn't sure what to do about Family Adrenalyn. She really thought she should go and support the KnitWits on the day of the judging. Even though it would be hard to see someone else model the blue dress, at least she'd see the dress in real life, and anyway, it was the final! She couldn't not go and help out the KnitWits; it was too important.

Azra jumped up. 'Your neighbour, Cassie! The one who lives upstairs. Doesn't she work for KW?'

'Azra, no—'

'But if it would help . . .'

They were right at the bus stops now, and it felt like everyone was staring. Cassie wished Emily was there. But she had climbing practice in the gym.

'Even if you can't get to see anyone else from the KW

label, you could see her because she lives next to you,'
Azra said 'She could be at home now, and—'

'Your neighbour works for KW itself?'

Cassie gripped the sides of her bag. 'The thing is, Holly, it takes quite a long time to refashion clothes properly. Especially when you're professionals like KW. And I'm not being rude, but I've so much on, what with—'

'It's not *you* I want to do it. It's your neighbour. So you can take this skirt and get it done.' She threw her skirt to Cassie. 'And that's an order!'

'What did you say?' said a loud voice behind them.

Cassie jumped.

Mira was standing right behind them. Mira was wearing her starry-sleeve jumper, an eye-catching hair pin and a furious expression.

Mira stared at Holly. 'I asked you a question.'

Holly took a moment for her face to rearrange itself. Bea did a little squeak, dropped down and pretended to be doing her laces. Mira took her hair pin out. It was long and sleek, with a blue thread tied at the end.

'I was just talking about a skirt.' Holly forced a laugh. 'I'm Holly and—'

'I know who you are,' Mira said, smartly. She looked at Cassie. 'Just as described.'

Cassie gulped. Azra's mouth dropped open.

Holly flushed. 'And then, I was saying how much I love the stars on my sleeve.'

'That's not what I heard.' Mira jabbed her hair pin towards the middle one on the sleeve. 'You sounded like you were giving out orders.'

'I wasn't.' Holly pulled her arm away. 'I love these stars! They were made especially for me by KW . . .'

Mira shot a look at Cassie. 'KW?' she said.

Cassie's mouth went dry.

'It's a new fashion label!' said Holly, sounding more confident.

Bea nodded. 'And it has already customized Holly's jumper, with an exclusive design.'

'KW?' Mira suddenly began to giggle. 'A fashion

label?'

'It's OK, most people haven't heard of it,' said Holly, sweetly.

Cassie's voice sounded shaky. 'It's just everyone was asking where my headband was from and needing to know the label, and then when I came back with the jumper with the stars on the sleeves . . .' she trailed off.

Cassie looked longingly at the bus stop. If only Emily was here, and not climbing the ropes in the gym. If only the cafe had taken longer to serve Holly and Bea. If only Mira had gone to the library after school . . .

If only the number 82 bus would show up on time for once.

Mira pulled her scarf more tightly around her coat. She seemed to have gathered herself together. She gave Holly a slow look up and down. 'Yes. Yes, I do know about KW. And you should be super grateful for those stars.'

Azra looked thrilled. 'Wow! All this KW stuff is so surprising!'

'It really is,' said Mira. 'So *surprising*.'

'And Mira Lal knows about it,' said Azra. She stared at Cassie, in a starstruck way, as if she'd forgotten Mira was actually there.

Cassie had never wanted the bus to arrive so much.

'I do.' Mira looked amused. Her voice switched tack as she turned to Holly. 'But you were talking about Cassie's neighbour a minute ago. What were you saying about an order?'

'Cassie's neighbour works for KW,' said Holly. 'She only lives upstairs from her.' She laughed lightly. 'So, I'm not asking Cassie to fix my skirt herself. I know she doesn't have time. But I want this neighbour to do it, and *that* was the order.'

'You were trying to give Cassie's neighbour an order?'

Cassie held her breath. It looked like Mira was about to explode.

But when Mira spoke again, she was super controlled. 'Cassie's neighbour is an extremely busy and important person. She's working flat out on a secret new design for KW which is going to be fashion's biggest win this year.'

Azra's eyes nearly popped.

'Well, then, maybe Cassie can—' spluttered Holly.

'And don't even think about asking Cassie for anything else because she's way too busy with her own work for KW.'

Holly stared. 'Cassie *works* for KW?'

'Haven't you heard?' said Mira, as she swept past them all. 'KW are working on an amazing showpiece, and Cassie is their new model.'

Holly dropped her raspberry chai on the pavement.

'I'm the model?' Cassie said, with a gasp. Across her mind flew shots of blue in every shade from forget-me-not flowers to the deepest midnight.

Holly and Bea stared at Cassie with a mixture of shock and new respect. Azra shrieked with excitement.

'Yes!' Mira waved her hair pin, like she was Cinderella's fairy godmother. 'You're going to be the *Girl in the Blue Dress*.'

*

Mira: I'm so sorry for landing you like that. But that Holly girl. Wow, Cassie. I just couldn't take it when she was talking about my nani like that. And I know I didn't want you to be the model for the blue dress so this is really bad of me. But it just came out.

Cassie: Mira! That was one of the best moments of my entire life.

Mira: Ha! Will you do it? Be the model I mean? As long as no one ever finds out what KW stands for, I think we can do it??

Cassie: I can't wait.

Azra: OMGOMGOMG you're a MODEL for KW!

Cassie: Sorry I ran off quickly. My bus was there, and I'd already missed one. xxx

Azra: I'm so excited for you. A fashion brand! You = a model. I need to know EVERYTHING. OMG, I just can't believe it.

Cassie: Yes it's very . . . surprising!

Cassie: It's sort of only just happened. I'll definitely let you know more when things are further on . . . but thanks xxxxx

Azra: My mum's given me a cafe gift card with enough for two hot chocolates. I'll come and meet you after you've done your modelling (scream!!!!) and we can celebrate.

Cassie: Thanks xxxxx that's so lovely. Just not sure what time I might be finished in the afternoon.

Azra: Plus we've GOT to do our uniform design this weekend. Don't forget!!!!!!!! We can do the starry sleeves (I think?) but we need the skirt or trousers.

Cassie: Haven't forgotten, I promise. I can't do during the day but could meet on Saturday after dinner? I'll ask Fern if she's free.

Azra: Saw her after school. She's going to get some waste fabric and sew stars on the sleeves of a Lost Property jumper (hope she washes it first!!!!) and says we can do the rest.

Azra: We HAVE to do the design. But with all the KW stuff you're going to be so fashion famous we're in for the WIN!

Chapter 13

'It's not only the sisters that are so beautifully portrayed in the film, but also the Regency costumes which bring a glorious dimension to every scene . . .'

Later that day, Cassie was lying on the sofa at home. She was watching a video about the top five films where costumes were historically correct as well as beautifully made. First was *Sense and Sensibility*, where Emma Thompson played Elinor, and Kate Winslet was Marianne.

It was just the thing that Cassie needed to calm herself. That and her new project, of course.

Cassie slid the crochet hook into the loop, wound the wool around it. She was finishing the strap of Emily's bag, with a tight stitch, that she'd read about in her history book.

'I promise to finish this new strap for your bag, even though I'm modelling a secret new design for KW.'

Emily was in the kitchen making pancakes. 'There's no pressure for you to finish the bag. Any time is good.'

'I love doing it, Em. Creating this is lifesaving for me.' She was totally in the flow of the stitches. Crocheting was such a buzz.

Emily gave the batter a final whisk. 'You might need your own life saving when you tell Mum that instead of coming to Family Adrenalyn you're going to model a ballgown—'

'She's already knows I'm not coming, and she was fine about it. Well, fine-ish.'

Emily had persuaded a couple of friends she knew from Climbing Club to go with her. Cassie knew that Mum letting Cassie off the family day probably had a lot to do with that.

'Yes, but she thinks you're going to the KnitWits, she doesn't know you're parading around like a princess . . .' Emily glossed the pan with oil.

'I do feel bad about it.'

'The modelling?'

Cassie pulled a guilty face. 'No! Not being part of the family team.'

'I'll tell them if you want.'

'Oh, thank you, Em!'

'I'll let it slip when they've finished building an emergency shelter on the Family Adrenalyn day. That way, they'll be happy and distracted and you'll have a place to live when they throw you out.'

'Ha, ha! But thanks.' Cassie went into the kitchen and cut a lemon into chunks.

'But are you sure you want to be the model?' said Emily, as she flipped a pancake. 'You didn't feel it was a bit off that Mira said it like that without asking you first?'

The Blue Dress. The Silver Trainers!

'What did you even say?'

'I don't know. Everything was such a tangled ball of words and emotions after school. It was a high-pressure situation! It's hard to remember how I felt when it happened . . .'

'Sure.'

'OK, this is exactly what happened.' Cassie went back into the sitting room, where Emily could see her from the door, and re-enacted the whole scene outside school. She'd already told her sister the end of the story. But this time she did every part from Holly's demands about her skirt to Mira's devastating reply.

'Then Mira turned to me and said,' Cassie flicked her knitting needle for emphasis, 'You shall go to the ball!'

Emily threw the pancake on the plate. 'Right!'

'So Mira didn't exactly say that last bit, but everything else happened!'

Emily poured more batter into the pan. 'So it's a yes from you?'

Cassie grabbed her crocheting. 'If you saw the dress, you'd know why. I mean, I haven't even seen the whole thing yet – it's still in pieces – but it's going to be breathtaking, Em! And I can't believe how lucky I am to be able to wear it.'

She threaded her crochet hook through the strap. Making something for Emily felt different from the stitches she'd done on her own headband, and it was a world away from doing the stars on-sweater for Holly. She had been forced to get that jumper right. But the difference was she *wanted* to get Emily's bag right.

'And it's a bonus that you get to skip Family Adrenalyn.' Emily dusted the pancakes with sugar.

'That's beside the point! Anyway, I'm still making your bag for it. It'll be finished tonight.' Cassie pulled a face. 'And yes, I feel bad for not supporting Mum and Dad. But I've got to take this chance.'

And that's all it is really, thought Cassie, with a sudden thump. It wasn't as if she'd heard from Mrs Khalid or anyone confirming she was the model. Mia had blurted it out. But that was just to shut Holly up. It didn't make it official.

For all I know, Leta's niece is getting measured up for it this very second. Or Allan got so fed up that no one has volunteered that he's adjusting the bodice to fit himself.

Emily sat down on the sofa, with a plate and two forks. 'Fingers crossed.'

The blue dress was finished.

It was hanging on a coat stand in the middle of the room. Cassie looked at it, her heart thumping hard. It was even more PERFECT than she had imagined.

Cassie's idea that the KnitWits stitched up everything had breathed new life into each piece. The shades shimmered, somehow more bright, more brilliant, more *blue*, now they were together.

The velvet bodice had a sweetheart neckline, featuring delicate embroidery and beadwork, which sparkled like sunlight on the sea. It was loosely ribboned at the back for style and comfort.

Artfully joined to the bodice, the skirt fell in huge dramatic sweeps, like waves on a fairytale ocean, scattered with petals and pearls. The feather-light georgette sleeves (the prettiest Cassie had ever seen) had a sprinkling of crystals, and the softly knitted shrug was gently placed on top.

Cassie's heart raced. *I'm so glad I didn't miss this! Just seeing it in real life means everything.*

Well, not everything, she told herself quickly. Her decision to come to the KnitWits meant she hadn't gone to Family Adrenalyn, and she didn't exactly feel great about that. This morning, while Mum and Dad were getting ready, Emily had mentioned the blue dress, and hinted Cassie had a special day ahead too. Their parents had been racing around with armfuls of wetsuits and flapjacks. But they'd wished her good luck.

Cassie's phone buzzed. She stopped gazing at the dress for a second.

Azra: **Just don't forget to meet me this afternoon! This is our LAST CHANCE to get our design ready for Monday!!!!**

Azra: We can't let Fern glue a couple of stinky jumpers together for our entry. We've got to do something great Cassie.

Cassie: We will. It won't be until later remember. I'm at KW just now xxx

Azra: So exciting!!!!! Send pictures!!!!!

Azra: Is there anyone there who does proper fashion sketches? Maybe you could get them to do one for our competition?

Cassie: Can't really, it has to be our own work. Got to go see you later xxxx

Cassie shoved her phone back into her pocket. She was trying to listen in to the conversation between Allan, Leta and some of the others, without looking like she was trying to eavesdrop. There was no sign of Leta's niece, but no one had said a word about who was the model.

The dress though!

It was like she could feel little invisible threads pulling her towards it. Everything about it made her eyes dance and her heart burst. She stared again.

You could wear it anywhere, thought Cassie. *The blue dress was worthy of everything: you could skip across a moonlit beach in it. Or step onto the red carpet at a glittering premiere. Or . . .*

'Reckon it'll look OK under the community centre lighting?' said Milo, from across the room. 'Should we open the curtains when the judge arrives and go for natural light?'

They had decided to model the dress here, at the 'very heart of the KnitWits', and Leta and Allan had filled in the final admin forms, now the garment was complete.

'OK, photo of the dress was uploaded, and I've filled in the competition form already, with all of our details.'

Allan looked at the time. 'The judge will be here in about an hour or so.'

'Time to get ready,' said Milo.

'Or to get someone ready, more to the point,' said Serena.

Allan looked nervous. 'As we know, our model must be someone with a part in the creative process; who believes in the project; who—'

'And like Mira mentioned,' said Milo, 'we'll get extra points because we have someone young at the centre of this, and the person who actually had the vision for the dress in the first place.'

'She's right.' Leta nodded. 'Part of the CommunKnitty competition was about sharing skills between different generations.'

'And you're completely sure, Mira, that Cassie wants to be the model?' said Allan. His voice sounded deeper and more serious than usual. 'She's hardly said a word since she got here.'

Mira pointed over to where Cassie was standing. She

had her back to everyone. Her cheek was against the bodice of the dress, leaning against it, with one hand stroking the sleeve.

'I think she's talking to it.' Mira laughed. 'She's like some kind of dress whisperer!'

Everyone exchanged smiles.

'Cassie,' said Mrs Khalid, gently. She went over to her. 'Are you ready to put it on?'

Nothing can prepare you for the moment you slip on the DRESS OF YOUR DREAMS, thought Cassie. As the fabric wafted and swished around her, she felt like a butterfly trying out her new wings.

Mira helped Cassie get ready in the loos of the community centre. She'd put her phone on the windowsill and was playing their favourite songs. Mrs Khalid kept popping in to check that every pin had been taken out, and to say for the umpteenth time that they were thrilled she was going to be the model.

Serena was in there too. She pinned Cassie's front

pieces of hair up with jewelled pins, so they fell like soft bangs over her swingy bob. After that, Mira did a sweep of eyeliner on Cassie the same as she wore herself. Cassie felt she'd never wash her face again.

Then, Mrs Khalid went and got the shoes. Cassie couldn't stop telling her how careful she'd be with every step. How she knew the trainers were not only super precious to Mrs Khalid personally, but were also an actual piece of fashion history.

'They are meant to be worn!' said Mrs Khalid. 'Just enjoy them.'

Cassie slipped them on.

PERFECT.

The hemline of the dress skimmed Cassie's ankles, and the metallic sneakers set off the midnight skirt. Every step she took looked like a shooting star.

She felt a flutter of nerves when it was time to go into the main hall of the community centre.

Mira was making it ten times worse by whispering in her ear.

'Cassie, the main thing you need to remember is not to say your name or our school or anything. If the judge asks you for details, just be vague. And say no to photos of your face.'

'OK, got it.'

'Please, Cassie.' Mira's hands were sweating as she opened the door.

'I've got this! If the judge asks, I've already decided to say I'm called Holly—'

Mira didn't laugh. Her eyes shot to where Mrs Khalid and the others were standing. 'It's not just us that people at school would laugh at, it's all of them too.'

There was applause and cheers from the others at the sight of Cassie in the blue dress. She did a twirl. 'It's your work that's so amazing! Not me!'

'Talking of amazing,' said Leta, after they'd all admired Cassie in the dress. 'My niece was sorry she couldn't be here, but she wanted to help. So she's asked one of her friends, Devan, he's a journalism student at the same college—'

Cassie and Mira exchanged glances.

Leta smoothed down her handmade shift dress. 'And the great news is Devan's offered to do an interview about how a community made a dress together.'

'Fame at last!' Allan said, as if he was voice projecting to the back of a theatre.

Leta nodded. 'He's going to write the piece for the student newspaper, but Devan and his friends will get it out on social. And who knows? One or two students have already had their articles picked up by the local press.'

Suddenly the ribbons on Cassie's back felt too tight.

'I thought this involved a judge having a quick look at the dress, here in the community centre,' said Mira.

Mrs Khalid looked at her sharply.

'This is better,' said Allan. His voice was so loud it made Cassie jump. 'This story could be what we need to get new members! Even if we don't win, this could showcase our skills.'

'And help you attract customers if you set up a clothes-making business.' Serena gave him a friendly nudge.

'I expect he'll want to speak to all of us.' Allan turned to Cassie. 'If you could prepare a couple of quotes on what the KnitWits means to you or—'

Cassie felt panicky. The bodice felt too tight. The skirt was way too much, even the trainers were rubbing on her heels.

'No way can you do this,' said Mira, right in Cassie's ear. 'We need to think of something before he gets here.'

Everyone was talking at once.

'Can we mention the traditional embroidery on the left shoulder?'

'No one point out the mistake I made with the cuffs!'

'Ooh, and Cassie, please don't say if the zip on the side is rubbing.'

'Don't stitch us up, Cassie!' joked Milo. 'Make sure you tell a good yarn!'

'Don't look so worried,' said Serena. 'We'll all be helping with the answers.'

'There he is!' said Leta.

Cassie and Mira looked at each other in horror.

The door opened and Devan, a student in his early twenties, came in, wearing shorts, jacket and big square glasses. He looked at the haberdashery table, the reams of satin and ribbons, and at Cassie wearing the blue dress. 'Am I in the presence of the KnitWits?'

Thirty seconds later, and Mira was shoving Cassie out of the door.

'Just go!'

'I can't just leave!'

'Hide in the car park or something until he's gone.' Mira looked stricken.

Cassie heard herself saying that she couldn't let the others down. She was sorry, but it was too late to pull out. She stared at the others. They were laughing and wafting pieces of blue material around. Someone had already made Devan a cup of tea.

'What are you going to tell him? That I've just run off?'

Mira was speaking in a low, very controlled voice. 'You have to. Just leave. I'll tell everyone you felt sick and needed some air.'

'What if we ruin the judging because of this?'

'You can come back in time to see the judge.'

Cassie grabbed her bag. 'Are you sure this is OK, Mira? They seemed really keen to—'

'Cassie!' Allan's voice boomed across the hall. He was standing with Devan, Leta, Milo and Mrs Khalid. Serena was putting the fabric samples back on the table. 'We're ready for you.'

Cassie's stomach twisted. 'Couldn't I just give him a false name, or,' her mind was racing, 'wear a mask? We could pretend this dress is for a masked ball, and then—'

'What are you talking about? We don't have time to make a mask!' Mira looked absolutely panicked.

'Everything OK over there?' bellowed Allan.

'Go!' said Mira, suddenly.

Without looking back – and still in the blue dress and silver trainers – Cassie ran out of the door.

It was raining hard. It was sudden and relentless, like someone had turned on a blasting cold shower. Cassie hadn't got her coat. She ran to the nearest shelter to save the dress from getting soaked. She stood there for a second, shaking the water out of her hair.

The old bus shelter had been there since the 1930s. The cream curved walls had lots of glass panes, in a classic art-deco style. Cassie caught sight of her reflection on all sides. Even in the misty, smudged glass of the old shelter the dress looked sensational. The bodice was smooth, the shrug as bright as a field of cornflowers, and droplets of water were clinging onto the skirt, like midnight rain. She could hardly believe it was her. *I was made to wear this dress, Cassie thought. That's not showing off, is it? It's the truth. I've never felt more fashion fearless in my life.*

Her phone buzzed. She thought it would be Mira telling her to head back. But it was Azra.

> **Azra: Remember I know KW is important! But we NEED to meet asap! Uniform design by Monday!!!!!!! Can you come to my house at 2pm?**

Cassie checked the time. She had about an hour.

> **Cassie: I'll try! I promise I'll come today. Know it's important!! X**

> **Azra: I've invited Fern as well but I don't want a rubbish glued up jumper. We need a real design! Get some KW inspo if u can!!!**

She shoved her phone in the pocket of her skirt.

There was no one around. So she dropped a curtsey

to her reflection. 'What, this?' She touched her hand to her bodice. 'Of course I'll tell you about it!' She did a little tap dance in the silver trainers.

'Note Mrs Khalid's faultless knitting,' she said, in her tour guide voice, 'which her mother and grandmother and aunties taught her.' She felt a swell of pride. 'And how well-crafted the bodice is. Who could tell it was once a pair of shorts, which danced in Paris? And as for the skirt . . .'

Cassie suddenly felt emotional. The KnitWits were so brilliant. She gazed into the glass window. 'And the real genius is that the blue dress is as comfortable to wear as an oversized nightie!

She heard a cough. 'That sounds like something I could get behind!' A woman was smiling at her. She had a baby in a buggy and a toddler standing beside her.

Cassie's hands flew to her cheeks. There were people waiting for the bus. *OMG! They've all been watching me!*

It wasn't just the mum and kids, further back there was an older woman, wearing a peacoat with dramatic cuffs and eating a pasty from a paper bag; a teenage boy humming a tune with headphones on; an old man with his hat pulled down; and a girl in her twenties with a side ponytail, purple tights and ankle boots.

Cassie cheeks were bright red. 'Sorry, I didn't realize—'

The mum brushed away the apology. 'Though you look more ready to dance at a ball than ready for bed,' she said. She ruffled the head of the toddler beside her.

'Don't stop,' said the woman in the peacoat. 'I was enjoying hearing about it.' She looked at the electronic timetable. The bus wasn't due for another three minutes.

'Thanks, but I shouldn't even be here.' Cassie's heart thumped. 'I've got to get back.'

'To a party?' said the mum, with a wistful look.

Cassie looked out on to the street. *No, to hiding in a car park to protect Mira Lal's reputation.*

Just then, the baby did a really loud, comic gurgle. He leant out of the buggy and pointed at Cassie. Cassie had to walk past everyone on her way out of the bus shelter, and she let the baby grab a handful of the skirt. The baby was pulling it quite strongly. Cassie crouched down to make sure the fabric didn't tear. The toddler was right next to her. She leant over and touched Cassie's shrug. She gave it a little stroke, then leant her cheek into the soft wool.

Cassie was stuck there for a moment, and while she was unsure of how to dislodge herself from the kids, the woman in the peacoat asked where the dress was from.

'Some friends of mine made it.'

'Wow!'

That led to more questions. But Cassie found it easy to answer them all.

Cassie knew about the different forms of beadwork, the spec of the lining, how many pieces the shrug had been knitted in, and even when the girl with the side ponytail asked some really technical questions, the answers came very naturally.

The rain had stopped now. The sun had come out,

giving the wet pavement a glow. It warmed the browns and reds of the leaves falling off the trees.

The mum was pointing out a rainbow, which was forming above the old cinema.

'Do you believe in fashion?' said the girl with the side ponytail suddenly.

'Random!' said someone further down in the queue.

Do I believe in fashion? Cassie traced her fingers over the tiny pearls on the skirt. Sometimes she believed that fashion could be happy, fun and daring. Sometimes she thought fashion was another way of pressurizing people to look a certain way or buy too many things. But fashion could be such a buzz! She thought of all the fashions that the blue dress represented – from the come-and-go trend for velvet to the heritage stitching on the sleeves by Leta. She wiggled her toes in the silver trainers. *Fashion means you can literally walk in someone else's shoes.*

'If fashion means being able to wear what you truly love, like this dress, any time of day,' said Cassie, 'then, yes! I really do.'

The girl with the side ponytail gave her a long look. Then she smiled. 'Thanks!' Then she slipped past the others in the queue and walked down the high street.

Cassie was about to do the same. The bus had appeared now, and everyone was getting on. Then her phone buzzed. *That'll be Mira*, she thought. She waved to everyone getting on the bus. *This has been amazing! I could not be in a better mood to represent the blue dress and everything the KnitWits mean to me.*

But it wasn't Mira, and it wasn't Azra either. It was a voicemail from Dad. Cassie's mouth went dry. Dad hardly ever called her. Her heart began to beat a bit faster.

It was noisy on the high street. The bus was revving up, and cars were going past, and now the sky had cleared more people were out of the shops and cafes. But that's not why Cassie struggled to hear what he was saying.

Dad's phone had kept breaking up. It sounded like he

was underwater. She could only make out a few garbled words. As she heard them Cassie's stomach plunged to its lowest depths.

Accident. Hospital. Emily.

She grabbed the side of the bus shelter to steady herself. The nearest hospital was on the outskirts of town. She looked at the electronic bus timetable. She wished she'd got on the bus with the others in the queue because the next one wasn't for another six minutes. *Six minutes! Anything could happen in six minutes.*

Her phone went again. She swiped it super-fast.

Azra: Are you coming or not?

Cassie didn't bother replying. She tried calling Dad, but no reply. She messaged Emily. She messaged Mum. She was feeling so distraught she didn't know how she was going to wait for another bus when a car stopped right beside her.

'There she is!'

'Stop the car!'

Cassie looked up to see Mira's face was at the back window. The door opened. Mrs Khalid was in the front, and Allan was driving.

'Get in!' said Mira.

'I can't go back there and see the judge.' Cassie's voice was shaking. 'I've got to get to the hospital. Emily's—' Cassie broke off. Her hand was over her mouth.

Mira flung the door open. 'Nani got a message from your Dad. We're going to drive you there.'

A minute later, Cassie was in Allan's car. He and Mrs Khalid were in the front, with Cassie and Mira in the back.

'Here's what we're going to do,' said Mrs Khalid. 'We're not going to worry about what we find there because it could just be fine. We don't know what's happened so there's no point worrying—'

'What did Dad say to you?' Cassie's voice was cracking.

'I couldn't hear him properly either,' Mrs Khalid said,

apologetically. 'It all sounded rushed, and maybe he was beside the river—'

Cassie's heart dropped further.

'It probably sounded worse than it is, right?' Mira said. She looked like she was trying very hard to sound calm.

The others were agreeing, and Mrs Khalid was repeating what she'd said about there not being any point worrying until they had more news.

But Cassie couldn't hear a word. She was too shocked. Too worried. Too fixed on getting to Emily. 'Sorry,' she said, a moment later when a splash of tears fell onto the blue dress leaving dark marks.

'As if it matters,' said Mira.

Cassie swallowed hard. 'I don't know what happened with the judge . . .'

'We're not sure either,' said Allan. 'She did phone us, said she was running late as she was looking at all the other entries. And then I got a message a minute ago to let me know she'd seen our entry, and she'd be in touch.'

'But she can't have,' said Mira.

'I know. There were lots of groups in the competition, so she must have made a mistake,' said Allan.

'I'm so sorry,' said Cassie.

'Don't worry,' said Allan. 'Let's just get to the hospital and . . .'

Cassie felt sick again.

'We'll know more about what's happened with Emily soon,' said Mrs Khalid, firmly. 'Until then, let's talk about something else and—'

'Thanks,' said Cassie, in a small voice. She stared out of the window, watching the buildings and cars fly by.

'We could play a game of *Name that Knit*,' said Allan, as he turned the corner. 'Sometimes it helps to distract your brain—'

'What?' said Mira.

'We played it that time the bus broke down on the way to the yarn museum.' His hands bounced on the steering wheel. 'I'll start. Moss cast on. Cable stitch down the centre with—'

'Cardigan?' said Mira. 'Scarf?'

'With a five-ply thread and they had to re-do the edging.'

'Leta's poncho,' said Mrs Khalid.

'Too easy,' said Allan.

'Anyone else want a go?'

Cassie's palms were sweating. Her heart rate felt too fast and all she could think of was Emily. Mira handed Cassie one of her earbuds. Mira put on their favourite album and they both stared out of the window.

At the hospital, Mrs Khalid took charge. They went through the main Accident and Emergency doors, and had to go to different reception desks before they found out where Cassie's family were. Cassie was grateful that Mrs Khalid did all the talking and worked out where to go. The corridors were endless and there were lots of signs to follow.

In the end, it wasn't really a ward. More of a wide corridor, with separate cubicles with beds in. There were long curtains around each area to create privacy.

There was a row of chairs along the wall. Mrs Khalid touched Cassie on the arm. 'We'll wait here. You go ahead.'

Cassie felt sick with nerves as she pulled back the curtain.

Mum was on a bench with hospital blankets on, her arm was strapped up in a sling, her hair wet, and there were cuts and plasters on her forehead. Emily and Dad were sitting on chairs, flicking bits of paper into cups to pass the time.

'Cassie!' Emily leapt up. The paper cups fell to the floor.

Cassie stared at them all. 'I got your message, Dad, but I couldn't hear you properly—'

Emily threw her arms around her. 'OMG! The dress!'

Cassie wanted to hug her sister back, but she felt a rush of confusion. 'I don't get it! I don't understand. Emily! We thought you'd been—'

Cassie sank down on the edge of the bench. She was relieved to see everyone alive and well – at least better than she'd thought – but she was so wound up by confusion, that her breathing was shallow and raced.

'OK!' Emily held her hands up. 'You take five deep breaths, and we'll tell you what happened.'

Dad explained that everything had been going really well – six families had turned up! – but near the end of the session, Emily had swung on a rope across the river, trying to jump down onto a raft where it was on a slope. Mum and Dad were already on the raft, paddling people across.

'I've done much harder jumps than that.' Emily looked upset. 'But the slope was treacherous. And I let go too quickly, hit the water and went under.'

'Emily!' Cassie felt a wave of sickness rise up.

'It's Mum you should feel bad for!' Emily shook her head. 'Mum dived straight into the river. She grabbed me and pushed me onto the raft. In seconds I was completely safe. But while everyone was helping me,

Mum was still in the water. She accidentally hit a rock, there was a strong undercurrent and that's—'

'When you saved me, Cassie!' said Mum.

'*What?*'

'I had my new climbing bag on me,' said Emily. 'You know, with the long crochet strap that you made . . .'

'Emily unclipped the end and threw it to me,' said Mum. She mimed the action with the arm that wasn't in the sling.

Dad nodded. 'Mum held onto the strap, like it was rope. That bag strap was stronger than anything we had on the raft. We pulled her in on it.'

Mum's eyes suddenly went shiny. 'I don't know how to thank you, Cassie. If you hadn't taken so much care and done those stitches so well, and thoughtfully—'

'The bag strap helped pull you out of the water?' Cassie couldn't believe it. 'The old historical stitches worked?'

'It more than worked,' said Mum. 'Getting me out that quickly is how I've ended up with a few scratches—'

Emily looked serious. 'And a broken arm, bruised ribs, bashed elbow—'

'Could have been much worse,' said Mum. 'We were lucky.'

The lump in Cassie's throat got bigger.

'And even though you weren't there, you were still a part of Family Adrenalyn,' said Dad, with a light laugh.

'But enough of that,' said Mum, briskly. 'You look incredible, Cassie. Apart from all of this—' Mum went to wave her arm around, and then winced. 'I hope today went well?'

Cassie leant her back against the cold hospital wall. She knew that nothing mattered apart from Emily, Mum and Dad being safe. A few minutes ago, she'd been worried they weren't, but now the intense fear had passed she just felt like crying.

'We've got to wait here until the doctor tells Mum she can go home,' said Dad, after a moment or two. 'Why don't you fill us in a bit? Tell us about your dress, and about school. We haven't heard about the fashion project for ages . . .'

'For good reason.' Cassie's throat was nearly closing up. So much had gone wrong since she started at Pipson High. Emily passed her a cup of tea, and slowly Cassie began to list all the mistakes she'd made since she'd started in year seven. It was a long list that included everything from the Shacket Disaster to inventing a fake KW brand to letting down Azra and Fern because she hadn't even done a uniform design yet.

'And I haven't even done my Maths homework this week!' Cassie said, in a panicky voice. Tears began to pour down her cheeks. 'I'm behind on everything. I've let you all down, I've let the blue dress down, I've totally messed up. I made a HUGE mistake about not modelling the blue dress.'

Emily looked shocked. 'What?'

'I ran away from the judge.' Cassie brushed away a tear. 'It's a long story. And I haven't done a uniform design for the school project. I feel terrible about that too!'

'What about the sketches in your bedroom?' said

Mum. 'They're brilliant. I'm sure if you enter them, you'll get some points for ideas at least.'

Cassie shook her head. 'Lots of people have got great sketches, but to make an impact we'd have to show our design on a real person. A bit like the blue dress.'

'I'm sure there will be other chances,' said Dad.

'I feel bad for letting Azra down, and Fern too – she'd gone and got piles of old uniforms to use for fabric. But it's too late now.' Cassie wiped her cheek. 'We can't sew a whole new uniform by Monday.'

There was a deep, throaty cough outside the cubicle.

Dad pulled back the curtain. Mira, Mrs Khalid and Allan were sitting on the plastic chairs opposite.

Mira rolled her eyes. 'You're telling that to the wrong people!'

Cassie: **Azra, I'm SO SORRY about not coming over to yours.**

Azra: Don't worry. Now you're working for KW you don't need to put your name on our design any more. I know this is just a school thing.

Cassie: It's not that I don't care. It's because there was an emergency. PLEASE can you come over to mine tomorrow morning? I'll ask Fern too. We can still win!

Azra: I think it's better to just hand in my sketches. I think I've had enough of trying to do this design with you. I've tried, I really have.

Cassie: Please come Azra. I honestly care about the design and I have an idea of how to create a real fashion moment.

Azra: I really think I'm done, Cassie.

Mira: Hi Azra! Cassie asked me to send you a message. She thought it might be better coming from me. Please can you come to the fire station flats tomorrow. I'll be there, KW will be there, we want to help bring your design to life and help you win.

Azra: OMG, amazing! Thank you!!! What time?

Chapter 14

The next day, the fire station flats were abuzz with activity. Azra was the first one around. She arrived so early she was there for breakfast. She'd shrieked for a while about how Cassie should have told her that KW was really a community knitting group ('I thought friends were supposed to tell each other everything!'), and Fern had looked impressed, but also raised her eyes at one point ('What's Holly going to say? She's been telling everyone she has a KW sweater'), which had set Azra off again . . .

But the second Mira arrived, Azra had shut up.

Not long afterwards, lots of the KnitWits arrived with sewing machines, knitting needles, threads and ribbons and trimmings of every colour.

Azra had her diamante notebook. She showed it to

Leta and Serena, while Milo and Fern piled the vintage uniforms on the sofa and table in the Coltsfoots' flat. Emily was making tea and toast for everyone, and Mum and Dad were saying they'd stay out of everyone's way while also being there constantly. Mum did give Cassie a pile of Adrenalyn pyjamas, though, which she said could be cut up and used for making the uniform.

Mira put one of the pyjama shirts on over her tee, and said the little pocket was actually a really cool design, and they could use it. Fern said they were amazing. She pulled a pair of the bottoms on under the gym skirt she had arrived in.

'We're going to have to put these ideas together if we've got any chance of making something we all love,' said Cassie.

'What have you got?' said Mira.

Serena, Leta, Mrs Khalid, Allan and Milo were all there, squashed on the sofa and sitting on the floor.

Cassie looked at Azra and Fern. 'So we've got the starry sleeves . . . the tank top, and—'

'And nothing.' Azra swallowed her toast. 'I've spent ages asking people what they want, and everyone wants a similar top, but some people want trousers, some people skirts, and those people want skirts of different lengths . . .'

Fern jumped up. She nearly knocked a vase of flowers over. 'Sorry!' She squeezed into a space beside the kitchen. Over the pyjama bottoms, Fern put one of the long, vintage uniform skirts on, and tucked it under her mini skirt. She did a funny walk, showing off each piece. 'So, what we're saying we need is something that looks like this . . .' she laughed.

'Not a problem,' said Mrs Khalid. She looked at the knitted tank top. 'You said you wanted a tank that you could wear on its own or over a shirt?'

Cassie nodded. 'Or with detachable sleeves?'

'And we want stars on them!' Azra said, brightly. She looked at Mira and flushed. 'They're just the best.'

Some of the others were standing up. Fern was showing the wrap style of the gym skirt.

'And if you do some cuts here,' said Allan. He pointed at the side of the skirt.

'And put in a panel around here,' Leta was smiling and nodding.

'You could make it a three-in-one?' said Cassie. She stared. The trousers were underneath the skirts. You could wear them separately. And the skirt pulled down a bit like a concertina to be a long, traditional skirt like the girls at Pipson High had in the seventies. You could also pull it apart, with a big detachable panel, if you felt like wearing it as a mini. And the wrap style meant it was easy to put in the different hooks and panels without them being visible.

Genius!

'Then what you'll end up with is a traditional uniform that can be customized for each person, whenever they want,' said Serena.

Emily was sitting on Dad's platform bed, swinging her legs. 'I can't wait to wear it!'

Everyone began to talk stitches and patterns. With

a few easy tweaks, they could add removable pockets, make a skirt into a skort, and add in puffed sleeves that could be whipped off with a few clever fastenings.

'I do love the tank tops though,' said Serena. She picked one up. 'OK if I mend this one? There's a few holes.'

Only a few hours later, Cassie, Fern and Azra were wearing different versions of the Pipson High uniform. They were getting changed in Cassie's bedroom – laughing and dancing with her favourite songs on. Azra was in wide swishy trousers, Fern had gone for the zippy little mini, and Cassie opted for an elegant, ankle-skimming skirt.

They all had the vintage tank tops, with detachable sleeves. For speed, they'd been made with the Adrenalyn pyjama sleeves, and Cassie, Azra, Fern and Mira had sewn on all of the stars.

'I love it!' Azra spun around the flat, nearly banging into the corner of the desk under Emily's legs. 'This is going to create a real fashion moment!'

*

Later on, when they were having tea and a cake that Mrs Khalid had gone to get from her flat, Azra suddenly looked at Mira. 'Didn't you say that KW, sorry, I mean the KnitWits, had a showstopper dress and that Cassie was modelling it?'

Mira flushed. 'We did have a blue dress, for a competition. That was *true* . . .'

Cassie flinched, as if she'd been prodded with a knitting needle. 'Until I ran away and wrecked your chances of winning.'

'We don't need an award to feel good about that dress,' said Mrs Khalid, firmly.

'Talking about the award, though,' Leta put down her mug of tea, 'I had a message from Devan. He seemed to think a blue dress *did* win the competition.'

'What?' Allan threw off his blanket coat.

'There could be more than one blue dress?' said Mira.

'But they sent a photo of all the finalists.' Allan was clicking his email on so fast it was glitching. 'And we were the only ones.'

'But it can't be us because no one saw you modelling in it, did they?' said Serena. 'You were in the car park because you felt ill.'

Mira kept her eyes down. 'Oh, Cassie, I shouldn't have shoved you out of the door like that.'

'Wait.' Allan frowned. 'You weren't in the car park of the community centre when we picked you up to take you to the hospital. You were at the bus stop . . .'

Cassie felt the room begin to spin.

Mira's face brightened. 'Cassie, did anyone talk to you at the bus stop?'

Cassie felt her cheeks getting hotter. She looked at Emily. 'Em! You know how I do those guided tours around my bedroom, like it's a fashion museum?'

Emily began to giggle. 'You didn't!'

Cassie bit her lip. 'Wearing the blue dress felt so incredible. Even at the bus stop! And there was no one there, when I ran in because of the rain. And I was talking about the dress to myself, and then . . .'

Cassie stopped for a moment. *Hang on* . . . After the

girl with the side ponytail had asked her what she thought about fashion, the girl had left the stop without even getting on the bus. *That was a bit odd, wasn't it?* Her heart thudded. 'There was this one woman with really cool tights and hair, and she asked a lot of questions . . .'

'Just let me check,' said Allan.

'Quickly!' Mira was on the edge of the sofa. She grabbed Cassie's hand and squeezed it. 'We need to know.'

'We all do!' said Milo. He waved a piece of knitting. 'Hurry up! I hate loose ends!'

A minute later, Allan was holding up a photo on the CommunKnitty awards website. 'This is the judge.' He showed the screen to Cassie. 'Do you recognize this woman?'

It was the girl with the side ponytail and patterned tights.

'Because it says here that she's Nisha Sharma.'

Cassie nearly fell off the sofa.

'Nisha Sharma?' Azra shrieked. 'As in *the founder of*

the tights empire?'

'I love those tights!' said Fern. 'The company is based near here! And they use recycled materials. Did you know you can send your old, laddered tights back too, and they properly reuse them . . .'

Mira stared. 'You spoke to Nisha Sharma? You showed her the blue dress?'

Cassie's hands flew to her cheeks. 'I just sort of spun around, and she . . . loved it!'

'She certainly did,' Allan boomed. His voice went up a notch. 'I've checked my messages and you won't believe . . .'

'What?' said Serena.

'Tell us!' Mira leapt up.

Everyone held their breath.

Allan sounded as dramatic as a voiceover for the latest blockbuster. '"We're thrilled to announce that the blue dress by the KnitWits was everything we were looking for in a winner. Congratulations! You have won the first prize in the CommunKnitty awards."'

Allan did a theatrical bow.

There was a loud cheer from everyone. Mira threw her arms around Cassie. Emily leapt up, and hugged her from the other side. 'There's more!' Allan held his hands up. 'The note from the judge says: "The blue dress was breathtaking and not only did the model know about the work and skills that had gone into it but she shared the best things about fashion. Like everyone else at the bus stop I was enchanted."'

Cassie gasped.

Mira did an air punch.

'Well done, Cassie,' said Mrs Khalid.

The others piled in with cheers, hugs and shouts of thanks and surprise. Cassie's mum and dad stuck the kettle on again and were rushing around hugging her and congratulating all of the KnitWits, Fern was leaping around, and Azra's fringe was flipping up and down with breathless excitement.

'What's the prize?' said Leta, eventually.

'Three new sewing machines and a year's worth of

threads and yarn. The idea behind the competition is to continue passing on our love of crafting,' said Allan. 'So we need to decide on somewhere to give them to . . .'

Mrs Khalid looked at Cassie. 'Any ideas?'

Chapter 15

'Well the day has finally arrived!' said Ms Ginty, in her *'Hello Glastonbury!'* voice. And in her bubblegum-pink trouser suit she looked even more cheerful than usual. 'The uniform redesign will be put to the people!'

Everyone was wandering around the hall, where the year sevens had displayed their sketches, fabric samples, clothes and accessories on tables. There was a stand near the door, where each class had to come up in turn and vote for their favourite design by clicking the picture on the screens. The results would instantly be counted and revealed later on.

Holly and Bea looked seriously put out to not have the final say or to be coordinating anything to do with the final. But Holly had her starry-sleeved sweater on show and was bragging about how nothing was likely to beat that.

Cassie loved going around the hall and seeing what people had come up with. Only a few people had displayed clothes. Mainly they were sketches, and mood boards, and pieces of fabric. One or two people had customized a shirt – someone had turned it into a festival-style fringed dress, and another had added sparkles to the collar.

And there was a pretty jumpsuit, a cardigan with rainbows painted on the sleeves and trousers with feathers down the sides.

Cassie, Fern and Azra all had a different version of their uniform on, to show all the options. Instead of doing a display, they'd decided to model their ideas by going around and showing people the different versions of the same outfit. That way everyone could see it in real life, Fern had said, and instead of hanging around a table, they could go and see everyone else's entries.

It was attracting a lot of attention. Azra's curls were bouncing, as she showed a bunch of girls how a swishy skirt could be clipped together into culottes. Fern was throwing her arms out everywhere and telling people about the joy of Lost Property.

'Is it true that this is a KW design?' Holly was suddenly at the side of the room where Cassie, Azra and Fern were.

'Not a design.' Cassie shook her head. 'Azra did lots of the design, and Fern had the vintage uniform idea. But we did have help from . . . KW . . . in stitching up the clothes.'

She felt the stars on her sweater. She stared at the tiny stitches and felt the soft threads that bound the stars to the fabric beneath. *Ignore her*, she thought, *we don't need an award to feel good about making this outfit.*

Fern leapt into action, and showed Holly and Bea, and others around them, how everything could be bought as a one-piece but you could wear it at least three different ways.

'And starry sleeves! Made popular by you, Holly,' said Azra, anxiously.

Holly nodded. She stroked her sleeve. 'It's a slight cheat to have KW help . . .'

'Oh, I don't know!' said Ms Ginty, brightly. She'd been listening in to the conversation. 'Other people had family members help them. Who says we can't have help from local community groups?'

Holly wrinkled her nose. 'Local community groups?'

Ms Ginty tapped Cassie on the shoulder. 'Do you have a minute?'

Ten minutes later and the results were in.

Cassie stood in the hall next to Azra and Fern, as everyone in year seven came together. *Win or lose*, thought Cassie, *today was a great day*. Ms Ginty had told her that Mrs Khalid had been in touch. The KnitWits wanted to donate their competition prize to the school, and had even offered to give textile lessons so everyone could learn to make their own clothes.

'It sounds fantastic!' Ms Ginty had said with excitement. 'I want to join in myself. What could we make?'

'How about the uniform?' Cassie said, suddenly. 'I'm serious! Why don't we ask if the KnitWits could help us all make the new uniform?'

'I'm not sure, seems a lot to ask,' Ms Ginty said. 'Helping every girl to make their own uniform is a huge task. I can't imagine anyone would willingly take it on . . .'

Cassie laughed. 'You don't know the KnitWits.'

Now, though, Ms Ginty spoke to the year sevens.

'What a display!' she said, her arm waving around the hall. 'What taste you have! What ideas! What cool fashion!' She whacked her smile up to full beam. 'However, there can be . . .'

'Only one winner,' mouthed Azra. 'Oh, help, what if it's not us!'

'. . . so many winners!' said Ms Ginty. 'Yes! That's right! In a way, you have all won, because details of what you've all done can go into your own personal uniform.'

Ms Ginty explained how Cassie, Azra and Fern – 'The original Fashion Dream Team!' – had made a uniform that could be customized and adapted into being pretty much anything you wanted. 'And if you like, it can even have starry sleeves!'

Holly held her arms up and waved. 'I've got the real things!'

'So, if we all share the basics, like the same colour scheme of navy and white, we can add in extras like detachable sleeves and skirts that can transform into trousers or shorts, we can have a uniform that can also be individual . . .'

Azra pulled at her sleeve. 'Cassie! We've done it!'

'In a way!' agreed Cassie.

Suddenly she was glad their design hadn't won outright. She didn't want to be the girl who told everyone else what to wear. She wanted everyone to be able to wear what felt right for them.

'And the great thing is, Cassie and her friends have been working with a community-based knitting and sewing group that some of you know as KW . . .'

Holly threw her arms down by her sides. 'Community. Knitting. Group?' she spluttered.

Cassie kept her eyes focused on the stage.

Ms Ginty was still talking: '. . . they're a super skilful group that one of our sixth-formers is also a part of. There you are, Mira!' Mira and her friend Bella appeared on the side of the stage.

Cassie's stomach flipped. She knew this appearance must have cost Mira. But Mira was smiling. 'They can make everything from beanies to ballgowns . . .'

'And guitar straps!' said Bella.

Azra was flipping out. 'OMG! This is the best.'

'I know!' Cassie smoothed down her own long pleated skirt. She thought of the times spent with the KnitWits, the fun of being able to wear what she loved, and thought that's exactly what a uniform should be.

'And they've agreed to come into school and help every girl make their own uniform. And what's more, they've given us the sewing machines and threads to do it.' Ms Ginty scanned the crowd for Fern. 'And Fern's got plenty of fabric to get us started . . .'

'The fashion revolution has begun!' shouted Fern.

'Come on!' said Ms Ginty, a minute later. 'Let's have a photo of the three of you. I know that everyone here is a winner really. But let's get Cassie, Azra and Fern together for a photo.'

They made their way to the stage. 'Lots of energy please—'

Cassie beckoned to Mira. 'You've got to be in this.'

Mira did a massive eye roll but she stood with Cassie, Azra and Fern.

Ms Ginty was looking at the stars on Cassie's sleeve. 'These sleeves are made from pyjamas, you said? How dreamy!'

'Lots more where they came from,' said Cassie.

'Could we call the stars, Pipson Version?' joked Ms Ginty.

As the camera clicked, Cassie felt a surge of fashion fearless. She slung her arms around Azra, Fern and

Mira. She looked right out into the crowd, seeing family, friends and classmates. 'Let's call them the KnitWits Version!'

'No one had been in here for years!' Fern pointed to the door of Lost Property. 'Until Cassie forgot her PE kit, that is, and—'

'There's no need to go into all that now,' said Cassie, quickly.

It was a few days later. The new sewing machines had arrived. And she'd had an idea of where to put them.

She opened the door. Mum, Dad and the KnitWits all went in first. Ms Ginty came next, and Azra was last. She was looking around the stockroom, her mouth open In shock. 'This is such a surprise!'

'It really is,' said Ms Ginty. 'But I'm just worried that it's all a bit dark and not going to be good enough. On *Sewing Bee*, they have those fabulous windows in the room they use . . .'

Everyone poured into the room and looked around

the shelves and cupboards. Fern had done an amazing clean-up. The bike was in the corner, draped with ribbons, and everywhere was swept and lots of boxes already sorted.

'And you'll really come here?' Cassie looked at Mrs Khalid, Allan, Leta and the others.

They were nodding and smiling.

'And teach everyone to make the new uniform?'

'We're looking forward to it,' said Mrs Khalid.

'And we can make it out of the vintage uniforms as well as our own,' said Fern. She grinned at Azra. 'This uniform is going to be on trend.' She did a big graceful point of her arm, in one of her dance-like moves. '. . . And historical.' She threw her arm out towards Cassie. '*And* climate friendly.'

Cassie laughed. 'The uniform of dreams! And I say that as someone who didn't want to even change it.'

Ms Ginty looked around the room. Her smile was so wide her whole face was lit up. 'Three new sewing machines donated to the school? So kind of you! I'm so grateful. And all the threads too?'

Serena nodded. 'Plenty to get started.'

'And we can show everyone how to use them, during Art lessons,' said Leta.

'It was a wonderful idea, Cassie,' said Mrs Khalid.

Azra was rummaging through the hair accessories box. 'I don't normally like old things . . .' She pulled out the butterfly clip. 'Ooh, this looks like one I saw the other day in a shop in town. Maybe we can sort these out and anyone can borrow or have them to switch up their outfits?'

'And we can still have some of the Lost Property stuff in a box,' said Fern. 'In case anyone forgets anything or wants to try on an old beret or gym skirt.'

Cassie looked at the wall near to the window. She felt a fizz of excitement. The wall over there was the perfect place to display the blue dress. The KnitWits had given it to her. *But it's a community-made dress*, thought Cassie, *and it belongs to everyone.*

Just then, Cassie's mum peered around the side of

a big wooden cupboard. 'Ade! Do you think you could shift this? I'd do it myself, but I shouldn't with my arm like this.'

Dad gave the cupboard a shove.

On the other side of it was a window, and part of an old door.

'Knew it!' said Mum. 'OK. We need someone to climb up there.'

Dad gave Emily a leg up to the top of the tall cupboard. She pulled open the old curtains, which had been jammed between the window and cupboard. Light poured through the stock cupboard. Even with the dust dancing in the air, the space felt fresh, new and totally different.

'How about we put the sewing tables here?' Allan said.

'And make that area a knitting corner?' said Leta.

Mrs Khalid nodded. 'We could stick the kettle over there.'

Cassie nodded. 'And we could hang some material

across here to make a fitting room.'

'And we'll help paint the place,' offered Dad.

Emily jumped down next to Cassie. 'It's like you're starting a real fashion house. If you want, I could paint a sign for the door?'

'Yes, please!' Cassie felt a rush of warmth.

Soon, she thought, *this room will be a kaleidoscope of colour from wools, material, beads and sequins.* Already, she could imagine the laughter, noise and the swish of the curtain as each girl emerged wearing her own version of the uniform.

A few minutes later, and the plans were truly taking shape. Cassie sat down on a box in the far corner. She ran her fingers through her headband and felt the stitches she'd made only a few weeks ago.

She thought about how sometimes in knitting the most beautiful garments are the ones that have been a struggle to make. There are twists, pulls and complicated patterns. There are dropped stitches, and bits that need mending and parts that you can't see how they're going to work together until right at the end. But that often they are the most brilliant, most important and in many ways the most perfect of all.

The End

Acknowledgements

Thank you to everyone who has worked on this book, and to my family, friends and neighbours for all the chats, fun and encouragement.

I especially want to thank my wonderful agent Claire Wilson, and my brilliant editor Emma Jones, and the whole talented team at Macmillan Children's Books.

My thanks also goes to the readers, librarians, booksellers, book bloggers and teachers who help inspire a love of reading in children, and to everyone who reads this book. Thank you!

Huge thanks to Mum and Dad, Donnamarie, Katrina and George for being total stars.

And finally, a million thanks to my husband John and our daughters Ella and Clara. You've taught me so many funny and important things about life, and about love, and I'm so proud of you all.

About the Author

Joanne O'Connell is a journalist, author and copywriter. When she's not writing (for national newspapers and glossy magazines), Joanne loves whipping up #noplastic homemade beauty recipes, from strawberry bath slushies to minty chocolate lip balm.

She occasionally pops up on television and radio, lives in the countryside, with her husband, daughters and their dog. You can find her on Twitter @byesupermarkets.